PR JAN 19

MW01102284

Canadian Historical ...

By Victoria Chatham

Print ISBN 978-1-77299-270-0

Books We Love
A quality publisher of genre fiction.
Airdrie Alberta

Copyright 2016 by Victoria Chatham
Series Copyright 2016 Books We Love Ltd.
Cover art by Michelle Lee

Funding for this Series provided by the Government of Canada

Dedication

Books We Love Ltd. Dedicates the Canadian Historical Brides series to the immigrants, male and female, who left their homes and families, crossed oceans and endured unimaginable hardships in order to settle the Canadian wilderness and build new lives in a rough and untamed country.

Chapter One

Monday, May 27th, 1935.

It should have been spring, yet snow still dusted the mountaintop framed in the railway station's open doorway. The pine-scented breeze wafted across Tilly's cheek and tugged a curl of hair from beneath her hat. Passing through that doorway meant stepping into a new life. The possibilities intrigued and frightened her in equal measure.

She hesitated, dragging her feet a little, as she exited the station. Now she was here, all the excitement and pride she'd felt at being accepted for a position at the Banff Springs Hotel evaporated. Despite the late May sunshine, chills rippled through her. Why had she allowed herself to be persuaded to leave? Couldn't she have found work in Medicine Hat or Calgary? There were hotels in both cities. But no, here she was, stranded miles from anywhere, still able to hear the fading rattle and clack of wheels on the rails as the train sped on to its next stop.

All she knew, all she had ever known, lay in a quarter section of farmland in southeastern Alberta, one hundred and sixty acres in sight of the Cypress Hills. Now the farm, seared by years of drought and the ensuing debt from one crop failure after another was—like her parents—gone, leaving her to provide for herself as best she could.

Her vision blurred momentarily. In the recesses of her mind came echoes of her mother's disapproval and her father's slightly softer, "Now, now, Tilly, tears don't solve problems." She blinked quickly to dispel them and squared her shoulders.

That's enough of that Matilda Margaret McCormack she admonished herself.

There was nobody come to meet or greet her, nor had she expected there to be, but that fact brought a sudden lump to her throat. The weight of being alone in a strange place bore down on her. She swallowed hard and took a couple of deep breaths to reorient herself.

The chug of a motor followed by the blare of its horn drew her over the doorstep and onto the boardwalk. She was too late. Her hesitation had cost her a seat on the last automobile that might have taken her to the hotel. It chugged out of the station yard, its horn blaring, and she watched with dismay as it gathered speed and disappeared from her view.

The hopeful butterflies that had assailed her stomach when she got on the train in Medicine Hat were now jangling nerves. How could she have ever thought making this move was a good idea? If someone walked up to her right now and gave her a ticket, she would leave on the next train and go home.

Except there is no home, she reminded herself. There is no family, nor anyone who would be happy to see her again.

She stood on the boardwalk and stifled the sigh that built up in her. Well, she was here now and would just have to make the most of it. The only form of transport that remained in the yard was a wagon being loaded by a young man. The ease with which he lifted and stowed boxes and trunks in its bed indicated a muscular frame beneath his open-necked shirt. From the style of his hat and his worn, dusty boots, Tilly thought he might be a cowboy. He was no stranger to manual labor, she could tell that. As if he felt her gaze upon him, he glanced over his shoulder and flashed a grin at her.

"Are you going to the Banff Springs Hotel?" he called.

Tilly walked towards him. "Yes. Do you know how far it is?"

"It's about a twenty minute ride but far enough that it would be a good walk otherwise. I'm headed there myself and can take you if you like." He heaved a trunk into the back of the wagon then turned to her, holding out his hand. "The name's Ryan, Ryan Blake."

She liked his friendly grin and twinkling brown eyes and took his hand in her own. He had a warm, firm grip. "Tilly McCormack and thank you, a ride would be much appreciated."

"Hop up then." Ryan indicated the driver's seat. "I've only a few more boxes to load. Is this your first time in Banff?"

"First time anywhere," Tilly tossed her suitcase into the wagon and clambered up by way of the wheel.

Ryan, having finished stowing the last trunk, climbed up beside her. "Where have you come from?"

"Medicine Hat." Tilly tilted her head a little so that she could study Ryan from the corner of her eye. The brim of his hat shaded the upper part of his face, but the wedge of auburn sideburn inching down his cheek and sprouting into day-old fuzz across the line of his jaw was clearly defined, even in the shadows.

"I hear it's been a tough time for ranchers and farmers around the Hat and across the prairies."

"Very tough," Tilly lapsed into silence as Ryan picked up the reins and slapped them on the rump of the patient old bay horse in the traces. Small puffs of dust rose up from the horse's hide in protest at this treatment.

Ryan guided the horse out of the station yard, yet Tilly sensed the animal knew its job well enough as it trotted along the route the automobile had taken. She glanced over her shoulder at the load of expensive looking trunks and valises in the wagon bed. Luggage labels declared they had visited London, Paris, Rio de Janeiro, Cairo, and Bombay. Places she had read about but could barely comprehend. Her own battered grip, a relic of her father's World War 1 service, fared poorly in comparison, but she imagined it had its own stories to tell despite not bearing labels advertising its journeys.

"Whose luggage is this?" she asked.

"The people who commandeered the transport," Ryan replied with a chuckle. "They're the first guests of the season and some of them will be in residence for the whole of the summer."

"All summer?" Tilly's mind spun as she tried to work out the logistics of staying in a hotel for three months. "No wonder they need so much."

"And the gentlemen often have as much as the ladies. They have to dress for dinner, you see."

Tilly didn't, and wasn't entirely sure what Ryan meant by 'dressing for dinner'. It sounded something of a ritual, but she refrained from saying so. Clean hands and a healthy appetite had been the only requirements for meal times in her home.

The wagon turned the corner onto a wide, busy thoroughfare that stretched ahead of them. Automobiles drove past them in both directions or were parked nose-in to the curb. People strolled along the sidewalks, some stopping and looking into the store windows.

"This is Banff Avenue," Ryan explained. "It's already busy, but wait a week and the place will be crawling with tourists."

"I can see why." Tilly took time to look all around her again. The soaring, snow capped ranges she had seen from the train had taken her breath away but now, closer to them, their sheer size and rugged bulk overwhelmed her.

"Impressive, huh?" Ryan's quiet laugh told her he had guessed the reason for her silence.

"Do these mountains have names?" She squinted at the mountain in front of her, noting its deep skirt of lush green trees. Having lived so long with parched, bone-dry earth she had almost forgotten how refreshing the color could be.

"On the left is Tunnel Mountain and that great tilted slab over there is Mount Rundle. That's Sulphur Mountain up ahead and Cascade is behind us."

Tilly looked over her shoulder at the mountain, which towered above its surroundings. Snow limned its treeless ridges and the deep striations that marked its gnarled grey shoulders. "I had no idea they would be so big. They make me feel a bit hemmed in."

"Coming from the prairies I can understand that. Cascade is over nine thousand feet high and is the tallest of them. It even makes me feel small." The horse had slowed to a walk again and Ryan slapped the reins and clicked his tongue at it. "Get up there, Boston. Move your hooves."

"Is it much farther to the hotel?" Tilly asked as the horse once more upped its speed to a shuffling trot.

"No, it's just a few minutes more on the other side of the Bow River and along Spray Avenue." Ryan turned towards her as he spoke, but she tipped her chin up and looked resolutely ahead. She wasn't ignoring him, but his close proximity suddenly made her a little nervous. "Not that that means much to you right now, being so new here and all."

"Well, at least I know about the Bow River," Tilly retorted. "It flows for four hundred miles from the Bow Glacier to the Oldman River and where they meet, they form the South Saskatchewan River."

"Whew!" Ryan whistled. "I guess you must have gone to school."

"Of course I went to school..." Tilly began indignantly, but stopped when his good-natured laughter told her he'd simply been teasing. She acknowledged his score with a smile. "Okay, you got me with that one, but I'm warning you I won't be drawn so easily next time."

"Next time? So you want to see me again?" Drawn by the mischief lurking in his eyes, Tilly turned away to hide the flush he'd brought to her cheeks. How could she have been so presumptuous?

A close cab, dark green Chevy pickup, reversing out of its parking place, caused Ryan to pull up. As they waited for it to drive away, Tilly spied a marquee, proudly advertising the Lux Theater, jutting out from a building on the next corner. It offered a promise of something new and exciting and caused her to utter a soft, "oh", of anticipation.

"Do you like motion pictures?" Ryan had not missed her interest in the theater.

"I don't know. I've never seen one," Tilly admitted. "But I'm sure I would."

"Wasn't there a theater in Medicine Hat?"

"The Monarch was on Second Street, but we never went." Tilly paused and then added softly, "I think my dad thought he shouldn't enjoy himself."

"There's our next time then." Thankfully, Ryan did not ask her to explain her remark about her father. "Once you've got yourself settled and know what your routine will be, I'll take you. The Lux is really popular. It has seating for a few hundred people and because of that, it's sometimes used for meetings or Remembrance Day services. Several motion pictures have been filmed around Banff, too."

She noticed the lift in Ryan's voice at this announcement. "It must have been exciting to have famous actors in town."

"Probably, but that was before I came to Banff."

"So where did you come from?"

Ryan laughed. "Not far away. My family still lives in Canmore. My dad's a coal miner but I never wanted to follow in his footsteps, so I got work at Brewster's. They have the contract to transfer folks from the station to the Banff Springs Hotel and back, besides offering trail rides and camping trips. I prefer being outdoors too much."

"I can see that," Tilly mused. An array of fine, white lines etched the corner of his eye and she imagined him squinting into the sunshine.

"But how come you know so much about Banff?"

"I ask questions all the time." Boston plodded his way across the bridge spanning the Bow River. "Right now I'm a packer, but next season I plan to have my guide's license."

"What has that got to do with asking questions?"

"A packer packs the equipment and saddles the horses for backcountry trips." Ryan paused while Boston made a left turn after the bridge. "A guide has to be able to do all that plus a whole heap more, like knowing the trails and all of his horses. He needs to have a good handle on people, or at least have a sense of humor, so the more questions I ask, the more I have to talk about, and tourists seem to like that. At least, up until now they have."

"Hm. That sounds like a lot to handle."

"Yeah, but I can't think of anything I'd rather be doing." With that, Ryan flicked the reins again and Boston snorted his disapproval. "Can you ride?"

"I've only ridden the mules we had on the farm, but I rode them a lot so, yes, I guess I can."

"You'll have to come out on the trails with me then. We have a couple of horses in our outfit that I think you'd get on really well with."

Tilly cocked her head to see Ryan's face.

"Practising your guiding skills on me, are you?"

"Can't think of anyone I'd rather practise them on."

They passed several big houses, set well back from the road and then, before Tilly had time to ask who lived in them, she caught her first glimpse of the hotel. Her jaw slackened and her mouth dropped open.

"Oh, it's just like a fairy-tale castle," she gasped. She had not expected to see such a massive building and tipped her head back to look up at it. Serried rows of windows winking in the sunlight studded the gray stone walls. Angled and steep-hipped roofs topped the corner turrets and peaked dormers, all reflecting the colors and rugged outlines of the hotel's surroundings.

"They quarried the stone for it from the base of Mount Rundle," Ryan told her.

Tilly laughed out loud. "And who did you have to ask to get that information?"

"A local stonemason I know." His grin told her he thoroughly enjoyed imparting this knowledge to her. "The original hotel was built of wood and what was left of it went up in smoke back in 1926 during renovations. The company covered the building with planks so that the reconstruction could continue all through the winter."

"You should write your own guide book," Tilly told him but then clutched the edge of the seat as he pulled up at the entrance.

Now that she was here a rolling sensation gripped the pit of her stomach and she pressed her hand against it, hoping the motion would stop. Nausea threatened to overwhelm her, but she took deep, calming, breaths until the feeling passed. She wished she could be as calm as Boston, who seemed only too pleased to come to a halt. He shook his head and snorted, then dropped a hip and rested a hind leg.

Ryan stepped over the driver's seat onto the wagon and had already lifted the first piece of luggage when three bellhops emerged from the main doors. It was obvious from the way they greeted him and the cheerful banter they exchanged that they knew each other well. Between them, unloading the wagon took far less time than it had taken for Ryan to load it. As the last piece of luggage was stacked onto a baggage cart, he vaulted over the side and down onto the sidewalk.

Tilly pulled herself together and dismounted from the driver's seat. White-faced, she leaned against the wheel for a moment.

"Are you okay?" Ryan asked.

"Not really," she admitted with a shaky laugh. "I had no idea the hotel was going to be so big. I don't know what I should do or where I should go. I just feel a little lost, I guess, and it doesn't help that I don't know anyone here."

"Well, for a start you know me...."

"But you don't work here," Tilly protested. "And where would I find you anyway?"

"Sam's place. It's a bar right here by the hotel and it's where the packers,—especially the Brewster guys—meet up at the end of the day.

I'm in there most nights when I'm not on the trail. The food's good, hot and plenty of it. If I'm out with a party, mostly anyone would know when I'd likely be back. And you'll soon get settled in. You're going to be fine."

His smile and his friendly concern warmed her and she nodded her head in slow agreement. Before she could say anything a bellhop with slicked-back hair and an amicable face walked up to them and slapped Ryan on the back.

"Hey, Saul. Good to see you." Ryan shook his hand and quickly made the introductions. "Tilly, meet Saul Gardiner. Saul, meet Tilly McCormack. Now that's two people you know here, Tilly. Who have you to report to?"

"Miss Richards, the Executive Housekeeper."

"Come on," Saul took her suitcase from Ryan. "I'll take you to her office."

"Thank you." Tilly smiled at both them.

Saul turned away, already heading for the entrance. As Tilly passed Ryan she caught a suddenly serious expression in his eyes. He looked at her for a moment and then, as if having agreed with himself on a decision he'd made, he nodded and smiled at her.

"I like you, Tilly. A lot. I think I'm going to have to marry you."

Chapter Two

"Wh-what?" Tilly stepped back, thunderstruck. "You must be joking!"

"I would never joke about a thing like that." Ryan climbed up on the wagon and took up the reins. "I'll see you soon. Better hurry now, Saul's waiting for you."

He drove away before she could gather her wits. She turned to follow Saul and couldn't miss the grin on his face.

"You are not going to be popular if he meant what he said," Saul warned her. "The local girls will want to lynch you. Ryan's considered quite a catch. Come on."

"Why would he say that he would have to marry me? He doesn't even know me!"

"Well, look at you," Saul said as he opened the door for her.

Tilly peeked down at her cinnamon-colored wool coat. Did she have a button hanging by a thread? Was her hem frayed? She knew the cuffs were a little worn and the pockets sagged as if they were too tired to hold whatever their owner dropped in them but, other than that, she thought she looked neat and reasonably tidy. "What's wrong with me?"

"Nothing, Tilly. Nothing at all." Saul's grin widened. "It's just that you're the prettiest girl to walk through these doors in a long time."

"Pretty? Me?" Tilly wrinkled her nose in astonishment that anyone should think such a thing.

Saul halted his long stride, dropped her suitcase and took her by the shoulders. He gave her a little shake. "Don't you ever look in a mirror?"

"Well of course I do. Every day," she told him. "But I'm nothing special."

"You have no idea, do you?" A look of wry amusement flashed across Saul's face as he recovered her suitcase. "I know girls not half as pretty as you who are twice as vain and try and lord it over everyone. I'll tell you straight, Tilly, you might have to watch your step with some of the male guests. The male staff, too, if it comes to that."

"That sounds very unlikely." Disbelieving Saul's statement, Tilly kept her head down as she trailed after him.

She knew she resembled her mother, having inherited her curly black hair that maddeningly curled even more in damp weather. She had her eyes, too, the deep blue of cornflowers. The shape of her mouth and her strong, stubborn chin featured her father. But no one had ever called her pretty and she still could not think it of herself. Sunk deep in thought she took in none of her surroundings. Only one fact registered with her, and that was their footsteps made no sound as they walked across what seemed acres of carpeting.

Saul came to a stop and knocked on an office door. After being bid a sharp "Come in", he opened the door for her and Tilly stepped inside. She cast a swift glance over wooden panelled walls hung with framed certificates and photographs. Two large oil paintings of different aspects of the hotel graced the wall behind an oversized wooden desk at which sat a smartly-dressed, be-spectacled woman.

As she anxiously approached the desk, the woman looked up and Tilly found herself being raked over from head to toe by a pair of piercing gray eyes. They narrowed ominously as they completed their inspection. Everything about the woman seemed narrow, from the tight, fashionable finger-waves set in her dark blonde hair to her thin, pencilled eyebrows. Her red lipsticked mouth pressed into a tight line, which did nothing to offer Tilly any degree of welcome. She placed a finger on the bridge of her spectacles and settled them firmly into place on her nose.

All the better to see me with, Tilly thought as she waited for a reaction.

"Thank you, Mr. Gardiner. You may go." Miss Richards waved Saul away as she got to her feet.

"You'll be fine," Saul whispered as he left her, but Tilly didn't feel fine. Her knees shook and she quavered under the woman's still cool-eyed appraisal.

"When we spoke on the telephone, I had no indication that you were such a good looking girl," she finally announced.

"Is that a problem, Miss Richards?" Tilly found it very hard to keep up with all the interest in her physical appearance.

"I sincerely hope not, my dear." Miss Richards took her seat and indicated that Tilly should pull up a chair in front of the desk. "I want to be quite clear from the outset," she continued once Tilly had settled herself. "Every summer, amongst our guests, we have very rich, influential people. Some of these people, especially the young men, seem to think they can take what I shall call...certain liberties with the female staff. You will engage in none of this behaviour. You will simply do the job you have been hired to do and nothing more. Our hotel policy is that the customer is always right and, in matters where there is a dispute between a guest and a member of staff, the guest must come first. Do you understand?"

"Yes, Miss Richards." Tilly answered meekly enough but her mind whirled. She supposed Miss Richards was advising her not to flirt with the guests, but in truth she wouldn't know how. Her only experience had been gleaned from the neighbor farm boys around her home. They annoyed rather than inspired her to any degree of interest, and she frequently left them standing in the dust.

"Now, you come highly recommended as a hard-working girl of good character." Miss

Richards held up a letter, which she quickly scanned.

"It was very kind of Mr. Bentinck to speak up for me," Tilly said.

"You worked for him?" A sharp glance from over the spectacles made her insides quiver.

"No, he was my father's bank manager and therefore mine, too, after my father died." Tilly clenched her hands in her lap. Thinking of that loss made tears prick her eyes and she blinked hard to prevent them from falling.

"What about your mother?"

"Also passed on." Tilly straightened up. There was no point in prevaricating so she simply told the truth. "I have no parents, Miss Richards, nor do I have a home. Most of my business with Mr. Bentinck was conducted due to the bank's foreclosure on our farm."

"And do you have any means to support yourself if your position here becomes untenable?"

Tilly sighed. She had been so grateful to the bank manager for his help. It had been he who had shown her the advertisement in the newspaper for housekeeping staff at the famous Banff Springs Hotel. He had allowed her to use the telephone in his office to make enquiries as to how she should apply for the position. Without his help she was sure that she would never have made the journey from a painful past to a hopeful future. But now that hopeful future seemed unnervingly dim.

"I have some funds available to me, but am I to understand that you don't want me to work here..." Tilly sank her teeth into her bottom lip to prevent it from trembling, "because of how I look?"

"I am sorely tempted to turn you down because of it," Miss Richards stated bluntly. "I think you, without it being any fault of your own, are going to be trouble. Against my better judgement, I am going to pair you with an experienced girl. You will learn how to service the rooms and suites with the Bow Valley view, which are occupied by our highest level of guests. Whether you remain servicing our top floor rooms very much depends on your performance."

Tilly almost collapsed with relief at this pronouncement, but Miss Richards was already on her feet, heading towards the door.

"Come along. I'll take you and introduce you to Felicity Jessop." Miss Richards held the door open and Tilly gathered her purse and her suitcase and followed her. As they left the office, Tilly heard her sigh. She stopped and gave Tilly a hard, unwavering stare. "And McMormack...."

"Yes Miss Richards?"

"Don't make me regret this."

Chapter Three

She set off at a brisk walk through a high-ceilinged service area and Tilly hurried after her.

"You will be working with Jessop under Miss Taylor, your floor supervisor." Miss Richards stopped in front of a bank of elevators, their brassware gleaming from frequent and vigorous polishing. "These are the service elevators and they are the only elevators you are permitted to use."

Tilly supposed this to mean that she would remain hidden from curious-eyed guests, but what would she do if those same guests decided to ride these elevators instead of the ones reserved for them. She counted the seconds it took reach the top floor, relieved when the door opened and they stepped out of the car. Through the windows opposite the elevators, Tilly caught tantalizing glimpses of the surrounding mountains.

"We are quite unique in that all our rooms are outside rooms which offer our guests grand views, depending on the weather and that, of course, we cannot guarantee." Miss Richards had not missed Tilly's interest in the stunning vistas each window presented. "You may well admire the view now. Once you have started work you won't have time for it. Ah, here we are."

They entered a room lined with shelves, each shelf stacked with linens and towels. A girl, who Tilly judged to be not much older than herself, counted sheets while an older woman recorded the numbers given to her. It looked to be a tedious, if necessary, undertaking. Both women's faces and shoulders relaxed at the interruption.

"So this is our new recruit?" The older woman, dressed in a neat black dress and with her hair swept into a bun on top of her head, stepped forward.

"Indeed, Miss Taylor." Miss Richards remained close to the door.

She can't wait to be rid of me, Tilly decided and, after the briefest of introductions, she found herself alone with the two strangers.

"Well, I must say you are not quite what I expected," Miss Taylor began.

Tilly lifted her chin. If her looks were going to be thrown up at her again she would have no compunction in telling them what she thought. Much to her surprise the younger woman, with a spark of interest in her tawny eyes, began to laugh.

"What's so funny?" Tilly demanded, fisting her hands on her hips and glaring at the girl.

"The way your face puckered up." The laughter subsided into a fat chuckle as Felicity controlled herself. "You look ready to spit nails."

"Felicity, that's quite enough, thank you."
Miss Taylor offered Tilly an apologetic smile. "I
can quite see why Miss McCormack would take
exception at being unfairly scrutinized."

Tilly slowly let out her breath. "Thank you.
It has not been my best day."

"No, of course not, and as it's late in the
day I'll excuse Felicity further duties so that she
may help you get settled in. I will expect to see
you both here tomorrow morning."

Their chorused, "Yes Miss Taylor", had the
effect of reminding Tilly of her schooldays but
her mood lightened considerably as they left the
linen room.

"So, what do I call you?" Felicity wanted to
know as they rode down in the elevator.
"Matilda? Tilda? Make it something simple or
I'm liable to forget."

Tilly laughed. "I can't imagine you
forgetting anything and it's Tilly. How about
you?"

"Just Fliss, but here's lesson Number One.
Our supervisors tell us it lowers the tone of the
hotel to refer to each other in such a casual way
so, when we are in sight and sound of our
guests, we have to use Mr or Miss Whatever.
And talking of tone," Fliss hesitated as they
stepped out of the elevator, "don't expect
miracles from our accommodation, will you?"

"It can't be that bad," Tilly protested, but
the suddenly glum expression on Fliss' face
silenced her.

"It's just that it's small and very basic," Fliss warned her as they exited the hotel and approached a group of nearby out-buildings. "Come on, here we are. We have to share the bathroom at the end of the hall, but this is home sweet home, or as sweet as I can make it."

Tilly looked at the travel posters plastered on the wall above Fliss' bed. The wall above the second bed was bare except for three hooks. A dresser had been squeezed between the foot of the bed and the wall. Between the beds, and beneath the only window, stood a nightstand with an untidy pile of magazines sitting atop it. She fingered through them. *Life. Time. Popular Songs*, and one she would be sure to tell Ryan about, *Motion Picture*. At the bottom of the pile she recognized the familiar yellow spine of a National Geographic.

She hooked it out with her finger and picked it up, observing it was dated February that year. Her father would have devoured it. She looked at the list of contents, which included an article on 'Petra, Ancient Caravan Stronghold', by John D. Whiting, and another entitled 'Silent Winged Owls of North America', by Maj. Allan Brooks.

"The guests often leave mags and books when they check out," Fliss told her. "Do you enjoy reading?"

"Love it," Tilly answered. "My dad and I sometimes used to read to each other. He would certainly have appreciated this."

She returned the magazine to the pile and looked at the bare, uninviting mattress. "Is there any bedding?"

"In here." Fliss closed the bedroom door and revealed, behind it, a battered old armoire. "I'll make some room for you, but it's pretty crammed. It's actually easier to store your stuff under your bed. I don't normally share, but as Miss Richards seemed to think you were some kind of wonder-girl, I was asked to give you the benefit of my experience."

Tilly sank down on the bed with a sigh. "Fliss, I'm no one special. Miss Richards must have got the wrong impression from the reference she was given. It really was a bit over-the-top I'm afraid, but I can't say I blame Mr. Bentinck for it. He was only trying his best to help me."

"Feeling a bit homesick?" Fliss searched in her purse and pulled out a packet of Chesterfields.

"I've no home to feel sick for." A tug of regret for all she had lost constricted Tilly's chest, making it difficult, for a moment, for her to breathe. It was hard not to compare her current surroundings with the tidy bedroom she had once occupied. She thought of the quilt so lovingly hand-crafted for her by her mother, the rag-rug beside her bed and the daisy-patterned flour sack drapes. She would have loved to have brought the quilt but had chosen, instead, to offer it to a neighbour's daughter. All she had brought with her were the clothes she needed and her parents' wedding photograph as a memento.

The crinkling sound of paper brought her out of her reverie as Fliss shook the packet and offered her a cigarette. "No, thank you, I don't smoke."

"Sensible you," Fliss commented. "Sometimes I wish I hadn't started. Fifteen cents a packet soon cuts into your paycheck."

The scrape of a match and the sharp smell of sulphur made Tilly wrinkle her nose. "How many of those things do you smoke a day?"

"Depends." Fliss inhaled deeply before expelling a long, thin stream of smoke, which made Tilly cough. "Half a pack usually, but more if I'm bored."

"Bored? Here?" Tilly couldn't quite believe that anyone could be bored in these surroundings.

"Oh, I wasn't at first." Fliss kicked her shoes off and stretched out on the bed. "This is my third season here. I mean, once you've been to the zoo and gone to the hot springs and on a hike or two, well, it's just not Miami. I must say I miss the beach."

"Miami?" Tilly's eyebrows raised in surprise at this announcement.

"Mmm." Fliss took another long drag on her cigarette. "Saul and I hate the winter. We've worked at the Biltmore and the Flamingo down there but are going to try for Hawaii this year."

"Oh, of course." Tilly sat down on her own bed. "And I'm going to fly to Paris and climb the Eiffel Tower."

Fliss ignored the sarcasm and chuckled. "No you're not. You'll hang out around here and freeze your butt off. Saul and I are going to apply to The Royal Hawaiian and the Moana Surfrider. Between the two we should get something and if he's at one and I'm at the other, at least we're not too far apart because they are both on Waikiki Beach."

Tilly, never having seen a beach, could only imagine what the combination of sun and sand would be like. To be in such a place with a young man beside her struck her as slightly daring. "Are you and Saul—well—together?"

"Four years now." Fliss responded promptly without giving any signs of embarrassment at Tilly's question. "I was working in the laundry at the Fort Garry Hotel in Winnipeg at the time. Saul brought us a shirt with a red wine stain on it. He said, 'any chance you can get rid of this stain?' and I thought, I can do anything for you. We've been together ever since."

"That sounds so romantic and a bit like my parents. Dad said as soon as he and my mom set eyes on each other, that was it." Remembering Ryan's warm brown eyes brought a smile to her lips. Could history be repeating itself? She thought not, but how could she be sure? She mentally shook the problem away and focused instead on the exotic-sounding places Fliss

29

mentioned. That hotel staff might travel between luxury hotels as readily as the guests had not occurred to her.

"So, how do you get these jobs?" she asked, intrigued by what appeared to her to be a very adventurous life style.

"Adverts in trade magazines as a rule but more often just word of mouth," Fliss explained. "But for that to happen you have to be very, very good at what you do. That's why Aggie paired you with me, so you can learn from the best."

"You mean Miss Richards?"

"Good grief, Tilly." Fliss hauled herself upright. "Of course I mean Miss Richards. Her first name is Agatha, but she's not here to take offense at whatever I call her behind her back." Tilly tried to school her features to be noncommittal, but Fliss had not misread her expression. "Oh, let me guess. I'm being disrespectful."

"As a matter of fact, I think you are."

"Don't be so uptight, you silly girl."

"Silly girl? I'll have you know I am twenty, so hardly a girl."

"And I'm twenty-two, so what of it?"

For a moment the space between the two beds yawned as deep as the Grand Canyon and then Fliss started to laugh.

"Oh, Tilly," she spluttered. "You should see your face. You really have to lighten up, you know."

"Well, I certainly don't want us to get off on the wrong foot," Tilly said. "I need all the friends I can get."

"First, we'll make up your bed and then we'll go to Sam's place. Here, give me a corner of that sheet."

By the time they had made the bed they were chatting as easily as if they had known each other for decades, not for less than a day and, when Fliss insisted on arranging Tilly's curls before they went out, she gave in.

This is what having a sister must be like, Tilly thought as she waited patiently for Fliss, showing a surprising flair for fashion, to tweak and twist her hair into place. When she was done, she produced a felt cloche hat and set it on Tilly's head so that her handiwork peeped becomingly from beneath its edge.

As they stepped out into the rapidly cooling evening Tilly remembered what Ryan had said about the packers meeting at Sam's place. Would he be there? She so hoped he would but, as they walked past the hotel, a rich aroma of something hot and delicious wafting from the kitchens made her stomach rumble.

"What have you eaten today?" Fliss asked.

"Not much," Tilly admitted. "Ryan said the food's good at Sam's. I'm hoping he's right."

"They have a pretty good menu, especially if you like Chinese food. The hotel kitchens close early so, if the guests want food late in the evening, they go to Sam's. It can get quite crowded. Not that we'll stay late, we'll have a busy day tomorrow. Here we are."

Fliss held the door open and Tilly walked into a dimly lit, smoky interior. Laughter broke the hum of conversation and mixed with the clink of glasses and clatter of cutlery. Men stood shoulder to shoulder along the bar, but only one turned to eye the newcomers. He removed himself from the crush and walked towards her, a smile on his face.

"So you couldn't stay away, huh?" Ryan's teasing welcome made her return his smile.

"Not when I was told there would be hot food here." She glanced shyly at him, hoping the light was too dim for him to see the tell-tale flush that warmed her face.

Fliss nudged her in the back. "Stop dawdling, Tilly. It looks like Saul has already got us a table. You can flirt with the locals later." Her eyes sparkled as she looked from Ryan to Tilly then back again. Her cheeky grin encompassed them both. "Hi Ryan, are you joining us?"

The look in Ryan's eyes as his gaze swept over her was answer enough for Tilly. A curl of anticipation in her stomach became a warm glow as she took her seat. A chair scraped back when Saul took a seat next to Fliss, then two more young men, dressed much the same as Ryan in open-necked shirts and denim pants, joined them.

"Tilly, meet my fellow packers," Ryan said. "This is Pete Cobb and Billy Nugent."

Both greeted her with smiles and firm handshakes.

"I thought Ryan here had to be joking when he said how pretty you were, but gosh darn, Miss Tilly, he ain't wrong." Pete's undisguised admiration caused her to blush even more.

"Knowed you had to be something special 'cause this ol' hoss took a bath this afternoon and it's only Monday," Billy added, making Tilly giggle while Ryan tried to quiet the pair of them.

Both Saul and Fliss seemed to enjoy the repartee and suddenly, without knowing how it had happened, Tilly sensed she had acquired a whole new group of friends. Suddenly her future looked rosy again. She relaxed back against her chair and pulled off her hat. In a moment of light-hearted freedom she finger-combed her hair, and tossed her curls back into their usual unruly mop.

A sudden spike of awareness made her turn her head and look towards crowd at the bar. A smartly dressed man lifted his glass to her and Tilly, without knowing why, shivered.

"Who is that man at the bar?" she whispered to Fliss.

Fliss glanced up to see who Tilly indicated, and her mouth tightened into grim line.

"That's Frederic Vanderoosten. He was here last year. Stay away from him, Tilly. He's nothing but trouble."

Chapter Four

"Why? What happened?"

Any answer Fliss might have given her got drowned out in a roar of laughter from Saul.

"Yeah, but Norman Luxton's a newspaperman," he said to Billy, "probably only telling stories to sell more copies of the *Crag and Canyon* paper. That's what they usually do."

"No, he swore it was true," Billy countered.

"So what's the story?" Tilly didn't miss the fact that Fliss, under cover of all this good-natured bickering, shifted her chair closer to Saul's and tucked her hand into his. It looked such a comfortable thing to do and made her think about holding Ryan's hand in a similar fashion. Laughter erupted again as Billy, needing no further encouragement, launched into the story of how the newspaper owner had accidentally started a rock slide.

"West of Peyto Lake he was, out with a group of friends hunting goats. He was crossing from one ridge to another when he got caught in a slide. Said a stranger came out of nowhere and helped him out, otherwise he would have been a goner. The stranger stayed with him until he was in sight of camp and then just disappeared."

"Right, Billy." Ryan waded in. "You'd have us believe there are ghosts in the backcountry, would you?"

"Ah, but that's not the only story," Pete butted in. "I heard tell that much the same happened to Jim Simpson out in the Athabasca River country. He got lost in heavy timber and a stranger helped him out, too. Took him right back to his camp. He turned around to thank him and there was no one there."

"Jim Simpson learned most of what he knew from Tom Wilson," Ryan scoffed. "There's no way he'd have gotten turned around, heavy timber or not."

"Who's Jim Simpson?" Tilly asked.

"You don't know—" began Pete in astonishment, but Ryan held up a hand and shushed him.

"No reason that Tilly would know about him," he said reasonably as he turned to her to explain. "Jim Simpson was one of the early packers and outfitters in Banff but the granddaddy of them all, is Tom Wilson. He had his start as a packer with a Canadian Pacific Railway survey team sent out to find a way through the Selkirk Mountains. Back in '97 he hired Jim on as a cook and trained him up until he became an outfitter himself."

"Yep, and shot hisself a record ram in 1920 too. That horn had a forty nine and a half inch curl on it." Billy sounded as proud as if he had shot the animal himself.

"So these are the kind of stories you tell around the campfire?" Tilly couldn't help but laugh out loud.

"Oh, I'm sure there are taller stories than that," Fliss said, "but they're probably not suitable for our ears."

A burst of laughter and several denials followed this, with Billy offering to tell them some good ones while Tilly devoured the pork chops and potatoes that Ryan had ordered up for her.

"And that might be true," Pete joked. "But what about that Ghost Bride up at the hotel, Fliss? Have you ever seen her?"

"Oh, that's just an old story, much like you've been telling us," Fliss said in an offhanded fashion.

"Out with it, Fliss," encouraged Saul. "We should at least let Tilly know what she's in for if she's to be working there."

"All right." Fliss finally gave in. "So the rumor is that a wedding party was waiting up in the library for the bride. When she arrived, they all went down to the Cascade Ballroom. Somehow, as they were going down the staircase the hem of the bride's dress brushed against a candle flame. I mean, can you imagine looking down and seeing your dress on fire? She was so frightened she stumbled and fell down the stairs to her death. End of story."

"Ah, but it's not quite the end, is it?" Saul's eyes were alight with wicked humor as he leaned in and crossed his arms on the table. "It's said," he continued in a hoarse whisper that raised goosebumps on Tilly's arms, "that she haunts the stairway and dances on her own in the ballroom. There are ice-cold spots up and down the stairs where she fell. Ask any guest. And some of the staff will tell you the same, too."

Fliss smacked Saul's arm as the others at the table laughed. "Take no notice of him, Tilly. It's nothing more than a silly story."

But something about the emotion etched on the other girl's face caught Tilly's attention. It wasn't fear exactly but even in the low, flickering lighting of the bar, Tilly saw her expression still and the color fade from her cheeks. Before she could say anything, Fliss picked up her glass, drained her drink and stood up.

"Come on, Tilly." Fliss grabbed her coat and purse. "It's going to be a busy day tomorrow. We should go. Will you walk back with us, Saul?"

Fliss' disappointment when Saul shook his head washed like a wave over Tilly. The gesture seemed so offhanded Tilly suspected just how together they were. She reached for her own coat but Ryan already held it out for her. She slipped her arms into the sleeves and he settled it on her shoulders, all the while fending off the good-natured joshing from Pete and Billy, who both teased Ryan about being a gentleman.

Stars were already twinkling in the soaring indigo canopy of the sky as Tilly and Fliss walked along in companionable silence. To her left, Tilly heard the distant gurgle and rush of water as the Bow River swept along the chasm below the hotel.

"You can often see the Aurora Borealis here," Fliss said, looking up. "Sometimes it's just white, but at other times the sky is as pretty as all get out when the lights are pink, green, and violet. The colors shift and swirl and slide up and down the sky. The packers will tell you that on some nights you can actually hear them, but I don't believe that."

"We sometimes saw them from the farm," Tilly said. "Dad and I used to sit on the porch and watch them."

"Not your mom?" Fliss asked.

"She died when I was seven, so no. It was just me and Dad." Tilly drew a veil across her mental picture of the past and returned to the present. "By the way, what was it you were going to tell me about Frederic Vanderoosten?"

"Oh, him." From her dismissive tone, Tilly took it that the subject of Frederic Vanderoosten displeased Fliss. "There's a few things about working in hotels that you should know. The male staff has it easier than we do, because they normally only go in and out of guest rooms when they deliver or collect luggage. We are there every day making beds, cleaning bathrooms, picking up clothes. If you are cleaning a single gentleman's room, make sure he is not in it before you go in. It has been known for a guest to open the door to housekeeping before he is even dressed."

"Fliss, you don't mean," Tilly's eyes grew round as the implication of Fliss' words of caution dawned on her, "with no clothes on at all?"

"I'm just warning you for your own good." Fliss shrugged. "Unfortunately no one warned a couple of new girls last year and there was a great deal of unpleasantness by the end of the season. Needless to say the girls were dismissed, but the culprit got off scot free. If you ask me, he should have been kicked out too."

"And now he's back." Tilly instinctively knew exactly to whom Fliss referred.

"With a fiancée, and she's no picnic either."

"You know her?"

Fliss nodded. "Miss Burma Evans, from New York City. Lives in a fancy apartment on Central Park West. Loves shopping on Fifth Avenue, Saks is her favorite store. Give her a chance and she'll tell you all about it, because Miss Evans's favorite subject is herself. She and Frederic are getting married here at the end of August but I don't see how they will stand each other. And watch out for that, Jeffrey Sachs, too. He's Frederic's friend and best man. You can't trust either of them worth a lick."

They had reached the door of their room but when Fliss opened it, she hung back.

"You go on to bed, Tilly. I'm just going to pop out for my last cigarette. I won't be long, so there's no need to leave the light on."

Fliss turned away and disappeared into the shadows before Tilly could ask her if anything was wrong. Instinct told her there was more to this withdrawal than just having a last cigarette. She entered the room and closed the door. The thin cotton drapes dressing the window were almost not worth drawing, but Tilly shut out the night anyway and turned down her bed.

When she slipped between the sheets and laid her head on the pillow, she realized how much the day had tired her and closed her eyes with some relief. At first the silence seemed oppressive, but then unfamiliar night sounds intruded. On the verge of sleep, the distant clank of a water pipe somewhere in the building jerked her awake. She took a deep breath as she identified the sound. Nothing to worry about there. A sudden burst of laughter and rowdy voices caused her to open her eyes again. A loose floorboard creaked, followed by shuffling footsteps. Was that Fliss? Tilly lay still, listening to each footfall but they passed right by the door. How long did it take to smoke a cigarette anyway?

She turned on her side, her back to the room, hands over her ears. She wasn't aware of falling asleep but must have done because she was suddenly awake. Not sure what had disturbed her this time, she lifted her head from the pillow and listened.

A stifled sob followed by a sniff emanated from the other bed. Tilly listened for a moment, not sure if she should offer comfort or allow Fliss her privacy. One thing was for sure.

Felicity Jessop was crying her heart out into her pillow.

Chapter Five

"Wake up, sleepy head."

Tilly groaned. It could not be morning so soon. She stifled a yawn and dragged her unwilling eyes open, blinking at the sight of Fliss, fresh-faced and already dressed. She groaned again and rubbed her eyes.

"I hope I didn't disturb you when I came in last night," Fliss said as she brushed out her taffy-colored hair.

Tilly sat up in bed, unwillingly threw back her covers, and put her feet on the floor.

"I didn't hear a thing," she lied. "Ugh, have I really got to get up?"

"Don't be grumpy. I gave you an extra ten minutes because you're new, but now you're going to have to get your skates on. Just for this morning I'll make your bed while you use the bathroom."

Rushing to wash her face and clean her teeth, Tilly couldn't help but wonder at what had upset Fliss so badly last night. Could she be homesick? Or had smoking her last cigarette been an excuse for something else? Whatever it was, the only sign this morning that she had cried herself to sleep was a little puffiness beneath her eyes.

Putting all speculation aside, Tilly quickly dressed, listening all the while to Fliss' instructions and explanations. They hurried through breakfast and changed into their uniforms. Tilly barely had time to admire her surroundings as they headed to the elevator, which whisked them up to the top floor. By the time they had loaded the service cart with linens, towels, and cleaning supplies, Tilly's head spun.

"You'll work with me today," Fliss told her as they stopped outside their first room, "so pay attention because you'll be doing this on your own tomorrow."

"What? No. I can't...I mean I won't be ready," Tilly protested. "What if I do something wrong?"

"You'll just have to make sure you don't. Now knock on that door."

Tilly lifted her hand but, before she could bring herself to connect her knuckles with the wooden panel, Fliss reached past her and rapped it hard. The noise echoed in the corridor.

"You don't have time to waste," she whispered and then announced in a loud voice, "Housekeeping, Miss Evans. May we come in?"

"If you must," came a muffled reply.

They entered the still darkened suite and Tilly stopped on the threshold, awestruck by the sight before her.

She had never seen such elegant furnishings and decor, such thick carpeting and lofty ceilings. Surely this accommodation must be fit for a queen. While Fliss half-opened the drapes in the lounge to let in the morning sunlight,

Tilly peeped into the bedroom. A swag of fabric hung from a valance on the wall behind the head of the bed, the soft, turquoise folds shimmering where the light from the open door fell across them. Lamps with colored glass shades sat atop the nightstands either side of the bed, whose occupant appeared as no more than a sleepy lump.

A froth of dark hair tumbled across the pillow as the girl stirred and sat up, frowning as she spotted Tilly.

"You're new," she accused as she pushed her hair away from her face.

Tilly found herself being observed by a pair of suddenly awake sharp, dark eyes. "Yes, I am. Today's my first day. Good morning."

"Would you prefer we come back later?" Fliss asked, but Miss Evans had already gotten out of bed and drawn on a feather-trimmed scarlet satin robe.

"No, do what you have to," she said in a resigned voice. "I'm awake now anyway."

Fliss started to pick up and fold the clothes scattered on the floor and Tilly silently followed suit. She watched Miss Evans from the corner of her eye. The girl appeared to be no older than Tilly herself, but there all similarity ended.

Tilly possessed a strong, sturdy build, but the robe draped over Miss Evans's frame emphasised her lithe and willowy figure. Her long fingers were slim and white and tipped with manicured nails as scarlet as her robe. Tilly suspected they had never been close to a cow or ever scratched a pig's back as her own work-worn hands had done.

"Tilly, pay attention." Fliss admonished in a vicious undertone. "I told you, we don't have time to waste. You'll never get through your daily quota of rooms if you dawdle. Here, strip this and put on fresh pillowcases."

Tilly caught the pillow tossed at her and quickly followed Fliss' deft instructions. If anyone had ever told her that making beds and cleaning bathrooms would be as hard as cleaning stalls, hitching mules, and plowing a field, she would not have believed them. By the end of the day her arms and back ached with exhaustion. Fliss simply laughed at her.

"You'll get used to it," she said as they walked back to their room. "Just remember, management won't cover your costs to go home if you decide to leave. They only do that if you're dismissed."

"Either way, that won't matter, seeing as I don't have a home to go to." Tilly flopped onto her bed.

"What do you mean? No home?" Fliss reached for her cigarettes as she sat down on her own bed.

Tilly sighed. "That's the reason I'm here, Fliss. A job and home all in one. When my dad died, there was no way I could manage the farm on my own. It was already in trouble because of the drought, and the one year when we thought we might just manage something close to a crop, the grasshoppers moved in and it was all gone again. There was no money to keep it going and the bank had no option but to foreclose. Without the manager's help I don't know where I'd be."

"Ouch. That's got to hurt." The cigarette Fliss had drawn from the packet dangled in her fingers as she digested what Tilly had just told her. "What will you do at the end of the season?"

Tilly shrugged. "Cross that bridge when I come to it. Who knows, I may follow you and Saul to Hawaii."

A mischievous gleam appeared in Fliss' eyes. "Not if Ryan has anything to do with it."

"What are you talking about?" Tilly pushed herself up on her elbows and stared at Fliss.

"A little bird told me that he asked you to marry him."

"Well your little bird is wrong." Tilly drew in a breath of annoyance. "What Ryan said is, 'I think I am going to have to marry you' and that is hardly a proposal."

"It is coming from Ryan." Fliss giggled. "Can I be your matron of honor?"

Tilly threw a pillow at her and Fliss, catching it, dissolved into outright laughter. "Give over, Tilly. Ryan's a great guy. He's got a good job with his outfitting company, and I know he works his own trap line in the off-season. Most of the local girls think he's a great catch, and you should at least consider him."

"But I couldn't marry someone I didn't love," Tilly protested. "That would be so dishonest."

"Well, I think it would be the ideal solution, and at least you would be able to be open about it."

"And what, exactly do you mean by that?" Tilly caught the pillow Fliss tossed back at her, fluffed it up and put it back on her bed. The sudden silence made her look at her roommate. The laughter had gone and Fliss sat pale-faced and tense on the edge of her bed, staring vacantly ahead of her. With dawning apprehension, Tilly remembered the tears in the night. "Fliss? What is it?"

In answer, Fliss reached hesitantly inside the collar of her blouse. Her fingers caught and held something then she slowly withdrew a chain from which hung a gold ring. "This is my wedding ring. And Saul wears his the same way."

Tilly reached out and touched the ring with the tip of her finger. It was warm from its nest against Fliss' skin. "But why do you have to keep it a secret? Did your families not approve of you getting married?"

Fliss shook her head and tucked the ring back into its hiding place. "They don't know, and it had nothing to do with them anyway. It was all about getting and keeping jobs. You must know how hard it is for women in the work place, especially married women."

Tilly nodded. "My mom was a school teacher. It annoyed her to no end that she had to give up her job when she married dad, and she never earned as much as the male teachers anyway."

"That's exactly what I mean." Fliss threw out her hands in exasperation. "We work longer hours for less pay than men, if we can even get jobs. That's why I started working in hotels. Men won't do what we do, nor could they survive on such low wages if they have homes and families to support. Saul and I got married two months after we met, but we kept it secret so that we could each keep our jobs."

"No wonder you were crying last night." Tilly moved from her bed and put her arm around Fliss who had covered her face with her hands. "That's awful. For how long will you have to live like this?"

"I don't know," Fliss whispered. "Saul has an arrangement with the head doorman so the better tip he gets, the more he keeps. We try to save as much as we can, but it will be years before we can even hope to have a place to call our own."

"Wait a minute." Tilly frowned. "If Saul has this arrangement, what happens with the other bellhops? Don't they get any portion of their tips?"

Fliss shook her head. "The lower down the ladder you are, the less you get. At some hotels the bellhops get none of their tips."

"But how do they manage?" Tilly asked.

"By the time they've paid for the cost and care of their uniforms, meals and accommodation, they're lucky to have a few dollars left in their pockets."

"That's awful." Tilly stared at Fliss, who shrugged.

"But we're in the same position, too. Until there's a union to fight for us we'll carry on working ten and eleven hours a day and consider ourselves lucky that we have a job at all. The sad thing is, that as badly off as we think we are, there are people who are in much worse positions. You, for instance. Tilly, I'm serious. If you've got a chance of making a life with Ryan, don't put him off just because you don't love him now. You don't dislike him, do you?"

"No." Tilly smiled. "Quite the opposite, in fact. But going from liking to loving and getting married is a long stretch."

"It need not be." Fliss shook her arm. "I fell in love with Saul right away and, however hard our situation is right now, I can't imagine not being with him."

A sudden thought occurred to Tilly. "So when you went out for your cigarette last night, you went to meet Saul?"

Fliss nodded. "That's what I meant about you and Ryan being able to be open. You wouldn't have to sneak around for the sake of your jobs, you could just be together."

But there was no enjoying Ryan's company later that evening when they wandered along to

Sam's place. There was no sign of him, or Pete and Billy. There were other packers snugged up to the bar but, because she didn't know any of them, Tilly didn't like to ask about Ryan. She sipped a cola while Fliss and Saul, holding hands beneath the table, talked quietly together.

She thought she should go and leave them to enjoy what time they could have together. About to reach for her purse, she stopped when the skin on the back of her neck prickled and a chilly tremor wormed its way down her spine. A fist of fear settled in the pit of her stomach and she drew in a deep breath.

She was being watched.

Chapter Six

"Fliss," she whispered urgently, "don't look up, but can you see if that Frederic fellow is anywhere around?"

Fliss made a great performance of stretching her neck, turning her head from side to side, then tipping her chin up and down. Saul raised an eyebrow at these antics until Fliss leaned in and whispered something to him. He never blinked, but the small smile that quirked his lips told Tilly he understood.

"You're not walking home alone this evening," he said quietly. "Just tell me when you're both ready to go."

"Take your time finishing your cola," Fliss added. "You don't want him thinking that he's rattled you. He's way behind you, to your left. Don't worry, I can keep an eye on him from here."

Tilly hardly noticed the liquid sliding down her throat as she continued to sip her drink. Her hand shook slightly and she chided herself for being so concerned. Frederic Vanderoosten could do nothing to her here with so many people around. Her fear was unfounded—it had to be. She had caught his eye once and been warned of his reputation by Fliss. Yet a persistent, niggling voice in the back of her mind warned her to beware.

"He's gone," Fliss said at last. "He just walked out the door."

"I hope he's not waiting outside." Tilly couldn't suppress a shiver as she pushed her chair back. Life had been so simple when it was just her and her father. For all the times she had wished for excitement and a life away from the farm, at least there she had been safe. She picked up her purse and scarf and wondered what advice her father would have given her.

"Well, I'm up to weight if it makes you feel more comfortable," Saul said as they left the bar. "I've done some boxing and I'm not exactly weak."

He pulled a face and flexed the muscles in his arms, making Tilly laugh. He kept them entertained as they walked back to the hotel and, when she and Fliss were back in their room, Tilly realized that she had not thanked him.

She had no opportunity to thank him the following day, either. By the end of her shift she was so tired that she did not even want to eat. Giving in to some not-so-gentle nagging from Fliss, she finally agreed that yes, she did have to keep her strength up, and together they went to the staff dining hall. There were new girls, like herself, and some old hands, like Fliss, but no one seemed to want to sit around talking after they had eaten their meal.

Tilly overheard a few grumbles about this or that supervisor. One of the serving maids had been reprimanded for not pouring correctly for a guest taking tea. Another complained at the amount of make-up she had to wear, and the time wasted to touch it up at regular intervals throughout the day. Someone else objected to the schedule they had been given that week, which made Tilly thankful that she and Fliss were working the same shifts. At least it gave them the opportunity of spending a welcome day off together.

"Come on," Fliss encouraged her at the end of her first week. "We could go to the zoo or the Dominion Cafe for a coffee or an ice-cream. It will do us good to get outside. We can walk into Banff along the river. It's quite a pretty path and only takes about ten minutes, unless we run into any elk. They don't always get out of your way in a hurry. A hazard of living here, I'm afraid."

They encountered no elk, only birds flitting from branch to branch in the trees beside the river. Tilly stopped frequently to look at the wild flowers blooming along the river bank. She recognized black-eyed Susan and Indian paintbrush, and Fliss pointed out a patch of blue harebells. They stopped several times simply to watch the river flow by. After all the long, dry years she had experienced, just the sound of it calmed Tilly. She stood with her head to one side, eyes closed as she listened the splash and gurgle of the water as it eddied around hidden rocks and boulders.

"You're really enjoying that, aren't you?" Fliss asked.

Tilly breathed in deeply, savoring the sweet, damp smell that hung in the air. "You have no idea how good this is after nothing but years of dust."

"Was it really that bad?" They had reached the center of the Bow River Bridge on the edge of the town and Fliss leaned against the limestone parapet. She had scooped up some small pebbles along the way and now flicked them, one by one, into the river below.

"Oh, Fliss. You have no idea." Tilly sighed and watched the light sparkle on the spray thrown up as the pebbles hit the water. "It didn't matter how well you thought you'd chinked the windows and doors, the dust still got in everywhere. It was 'wash this and dust' that all the time and you couldn't leave food uncovered for a moment. Dad and I were going into Medicine Hat one day. He wasn't even sure if the pick-up would start, it used to get so choked with dirt. But when it did we just sat there, watching the dust dance across the hood and form patterns from the vibration of the motor. But the dust storms were the worst."

"I heard about those." Fliss sent her last pebble spinning into the water. "I'm glad I've never seen one."

"I hope you never see one either. You think the end of the world is coming. It starts off as a dark smudge on the horizon that gets higher as it gets closer. It seems as if each side of it is curling around you, and then, if you haven't already run for cover, it's too late. You are engulfed by thick, choking, clouds of dirt that sting your skin and get into your clothes."

"I guess, living in a city, I never really knew it could be that bad," Fliss said quietly.

"No." Tilly shook her head, as if to drive the memory away. "Unless you lived it, it's hard to understand how bad it was."

"But all that's behind you now. Come on." Fliss grabbed Tilly's arm and pulled her across the road to the other side of the bridge and pointed out the various enclosures they could see in the zoo. "Would like to start here?"

Before Tilly could decide, she spotted a familiar figure driving a horse and wagon towards them. Her heart gave an unexpected lurch of happiness, and without giving any thought to it she waved. Ryan pulled up beside them.

"Hello, ladies." He tipped his hat to them. "Where are you off to?"

"We hadn't decided," Tilly said, unable to keep a smile off her face as she looked up at him.

"Why don't you come out to the Cave and Basin with me?" He scootched across the driver's seat and patted the space beside him. "There's room for you both."

Tilly didn't hesitate and quickly clambered up onto the wagon. Her heart beat a little faster at the smile in his eyes and the curve of his lips. It was a welcome just for her and she felt the blush rising in her cheeks. To hide her sudden shyness she quickly turned to offer her hand to Fliss, who shook her head and laughed.

"You go on," she said, hanging back. "I've got to shop for a few things anyway. Get a move on, Ryan, you're causing a traffic jam."

Tilly looked back as the wagon moved off. "I feel a bit bad about leaving her. It's her day off, too, and we had planned to spend it together."

"Don't worry about Fliss. She knows Banff well enough not to be at a loss for long. Where were you going anyway?"

"We hadn't actually decided," Tilly admitted. "Fliss mentioned the zoo. I've never been to one, and thought that would be as good a place to go as any. It's a nice day to be outside."

"The zoo isn't what it used to be," Ryan said. "Now that it's easy enough for tourists to see animals like bears and Rocky Mountain sheep along the highways and railway tracks, there's not much point in keeping them in enclosures. They still have some wolves and coyotes and a few fancy birds in the aviary, and the polar bear, Buddy. He's been a great attraction over the years."

"It somehow doesn't seem right to me to keep animals in cages," Tilly mused.

"I guess it all depends on your perspective," Ryan said. "I don't like being confined myself, so I tend to agree with you, but when the zoo was first built it was considered to be ahead of its time. All the cages had water flowing through them and good drainage, so the animals were clean and well kept."

Suddenly Tilly started to giggle. "Go on," she said. "Now tell me that you know one of the keepers there."

Ryan laughed with her. "Actually, I do. And not just one but two of them. But you should go. It's worth taking a look and make sure to tour through the museum, too. They've got some fine exhibits and it's actually as world famous as the hotel."

Ryan turned right at the end of the bridge, taking the opposite direction to the first time he had taken her up on the wagon. Once Boston had his bearings and settled into a steady trot, Ryan nudged Tilly's arm.

"That's the Sign of the Goat Curio Shop over there. Mr. Luxton has the local Stoney Indians bring in their crafts and sell them there."

"Hmm." Tilly looked over her shoulder at the building as the wagon rolled by. "Mr. Luxton's name seems to turn up all the time."

"That's because he's done so much to help establish the town. It's come a long way from when it was only Railway Siding Number Twenty-Nine."

"Why Twenty-Nine?" Tilly asked.

Ryan grinned at her. "Back then there was no town, only a railway work camp and it was the twenty-ninth siding west of Medicine Hat on the Canadian Pacific Railway line. Seems quite fitting that you're here now."

They passed several houses and Tilly peeked past Ryan to look at them. They must have a good view of the river, she thought. Its constant flow almost mesmerised her and she couldn't imagine it being the first thing she saw every morning. A creek had run along the southwest boundary of their farm, but through the years of the drought it had shrunk to a muddy trickle.

"So what's this Cave and Basin place we're going to?" she asked when she finally drew her attention away from the river.

"It's what made Banff famous," Ryan told her. "The cave is the site of the hot springs. The basin is the original thermal pool, and now there's a swimming pool as well."

"And you're going to tell me all about it?"

The smile became a chuckle and Ryan shook his head. "Only if you want me to."

"I do." Without thinking, Tilly placed her hand on his arm. He looked down at it then covered it with his own.

"I like the sound of that," he said softly.

Tilly shivered, suddenly remembering the first day she had met him and he said he would have to marry her. She tried to withdraw her hand, but he continued to hold it.

"You've got good, honest hands. I like that." His smile lit up his whole face and sent Tilly's pulse in to overdrive. "And I'm still going to marry you."

Chapter Seven

"But you don't even know me," she protested, still bewildered that Ryan could be so positive of his future when she could not begin to imagine hers.

"I know all I want to know for now." Ryan still held her hand and gave it a squeeze. "Don't worry, everything will work out fine."

Tilly shook her head, making her black curls dance. "You are an impossible dreamer."

"Better to be a dreamer than to have no dreams at all. Hup, Boston."

He flicked the reins and the horse leaned into his collar as he headed up a steep stretch of road. Tilly looked up to the building above her, which Ryan told her was the swimming pool. She thought the red-tiled pagoda-style turrets at the entrance had a foreign, exotic, appearance. Shouts of laughter and the sound of water splashing drifted over the high stone wall enclosing the area.

"When I've dropped off this delivery I'll show you the springs and the cave," he said as he pulled up outside a service entrance gate.

"How can you do that when you don't even work here?" Tilly demanded. As soon as the words were out of her mouth realization hit her. "Oh. Don't tell me. You know somebody who does."

"Of course I do." Ryan chuckled as Tilly rolled her eyes. "Several somebodies, in fact, but especially Scotty Sutherland. He's been a life-guard here for I don't know how long. You'll like him."

While Ryan unloaded the wagon, Tilly chatted with Scotty, not surprised to find that she did like him. She had yet not to like any of the people Ryan had introduced her to so far. When he was done, he looked up at the hillside behind them.

"We have to go up there," he said, pointing to the faint outline of a trail. "It's a bit of a scramble, but I think you'll manage."

The sun beat down on the back of her neck as she followed Ryan up the steep track. She stumbled and the sound of gravel skittering off the path made him turn to her. Without a word he held out his hand and she took it, surprised at how satisfying a sensation it was to have her hand gripped by his larger one.

"It stinks of rotten eggs." The steamy, moist air that hung beneath the trees and filtered through the scrub in diaphanous clouds almost choked her.

"That's the sulphur. Some days it smells worse than others." Ryan came to a stop and pulled Tilly to his side. "Do you trust me?"

Surprised, Tilly looked up at him. Despite being shaded by the brim of his hat, she clearly saw the slightly anxious expression in his eyes as he awaited her answer. "It never occurred to me not to."

"Then close your eyes."

She did and shivered as his hands gently cupped her shoulders and turned her around. The ground beneath her toes dipped away. She had an overwhelming sensation of falling. Was that why he asked if she trusted him? She breathed in deeply, concentrating on the weight of his hands on her shoulders, the closeness of his body behind her. No, he wouldn't let her fall, but what was he going to do?

"Now open your eyes." His whisper in her ear sent tingles down her spine, but that wasn't what brought a gasp of surprise to her lips.

From where they stood she could see from one end of the deep, green valley nestled between the crags, to the other. The hazy bulk of Tunnel Mountain shimmered in the distance and beyond it stretched range after range of mountains for which she did not have names. Narrowing her eyes against the strong sunlight, she squinted across the pool complex below her to the long chain of mountains on the far side of the river. A train, pulling a long line of freight cars, rumbled past and just beyond the railway line the glint of sunshine on glass indicated traffic on the highway.

"Oh, this is spectacular," Tilly said on a sigh. "No wonder people come from all over the world to see this place."

Standing beside her Ryan, obviously delighted with her reaction, nodded his agreement. "That's what William Van Horne intended."

"You'd better tell me all about him," Tilly invited but chuckled as she added, "just so you can continue to practice your conversational skills of course. I wouldn't want you to fail the grade on the subject."

"Aren't you the cheeky one?" Ryan laughed and tapped the end of her nose with his forefinger. The intimate little gesture caused heat to rush into Tilly's cheeks. She blushed even more when she looked up into his eyes and saw the soft expression in them. His smile was gentle as his gaze travelled over the contours of her face. "And even prettier when you blush."

"Oh, I hate that I do." Tilly closed her eyes and shook her head. "It makes me feel like I'm twelve years old, not twenty."

"Thank you," he said. "Now I don't have to ask you how old you are."

For a moment Tilly hesitated. She feared she might be flirting in the way Miss Richards had warned her against but then gazed at Ryan from under her lashes and asked, "What about you?"

"Oh, as old as my tongue and younger than my teeth I reckon." His eyes danced with merriment as Tilly tightened her lips and puffed out her cheeks, but then he took pity on her frustration. "Fair's fair, I suppose. I'm twenty-three next Friday."

She thanked him for that information but then insisted that he continue with his story. Ryan glanced around and spotted a fallen tree-trunk.

"Come and sit down," he invited, brushing debris off the bark. Once Tilly had made herself comfortable, he took up his narrative. "William Van Horne had a reputation of being a big man with big ideas and was a railway man through and through. He came up from the United States in '82 to head up the CPR in Canada. By all accounts he wasn't the easiest character to deal with, but he got things done. He reckoned that if he couldn't export the scenery from here, he'd import the tourists. It was his idea to build a chain of luxury hotels along the line. He was something of an architect too, and came up with the designs for the hotels."

"I've only heard about the Banff Springs Hotel," Tilly said. "Where are the others?"

"There's the Mount Stephen House at Field, the Fraser Canyon Hotel at North Bend, and Glacier House up in the Rogers Pass, all built to attract the wealthiest guests."

"Well, as interesting as that is, what has all that got to do with the Cave and Basin?" Tilly's brow wrinkled in thought as she tried to connect the two threads of his story.

"When the railway came through, all these mountains had to be surveyed to determine the best route for the railway. Surveyors carry an awful lot of gear and that's when the packers started getting real busy. They, and railroad workers, were scouting all through these mountains for years and here's the exciting part, Tilly," Ryan took her hand, stood up and guided her towards a steaming hole in the ground. She held on tight to his hand as she peered into the depths. "The Indians had known about these hot springs for centuries, but it wasn't until '83 that three railroad workers found it. Can you imagine coming across this vent and wondering what was down there? Brothers William and Tom McCardell and their friend Frank McCabe certainly did."

"But how did they get down there?" Tilly wrinkled her nose at the strong smell of sulphur rising from the hole.

"They dropped a tree through the vent then shinnied down it, using it like a ladder. There was enough light for them to see the pool at the bottom and a bit of the cavern around it."

"So what did they do then?" Tilly finally drew back from the edge, having seen as much as she could in the dim interior.

"Well, although they worked for the CPR, they decided to make some money from their find. They staked off an area around the site, built a log cabin close by to use as the entrance, and started charging folks to come see it, but that didn't last."

"Why not?" In spite of herself, Ryan's enthusiasm for his story intrigued her.

"Ah, well," Ryan continued, really warming to his subject now. "The claim was in dispute from the get-go. That led to the government getting involved, especially after the McCardell's and McCabe showed the site to William Pearce, who was the Superintendent of Mines at the time.

"Now, Van Horne had already spoken to Pearce about setting up a national park system. Early in '85 Pearce talked to Thomas White, the Minister for the Interior, about Van Horne's idea. Later that year, White called Pearce to Ottawa and on November 25th, 1885 the Federal Government established a ten square mile site as the Banff Hot Springs Reserve."

"And the town and the hotel grew because of these springs?" Tilly could now see where the story was heading.

"They sure did," Ryan enthused. "The government went on to extend the original area of the park and White and Pearce then suggested that if the town-site had a sanitarium near the springs, it could be advertised like European spas." He shrugged, as if the idea was obvious and simple. "It worked. It brought people here in droves. And what's more, two years later in '87, the government extended the park again and called it the Rocky Mountains Park, making it the first national park in Canada. It wasn't known as Banff National Park until a few years ago when the National Parks Act took effect in 1930."

"All this information is making my head spin." Tilly put her hands over her ears and grinned at him. "Where do you learn all this stuff?"

"I read a lot and—"

"You ask questions," Tilly finished for him, laughing.

"Come on." Ryan didn't seem at all perturbed by her teasing. "Are you ready to see the cave now?"

Chapter Eight

Tilly nodded and set out behind him down the steep trail, noting how easily he avoided tree roots or small rocks. It was as if his feet had a mind and eyes of their own, and the rest of his body simply followed their lead. She wished she had his sure-footedness and, as if sensing her faltering steps, he stopped and waited for her.

His smile encouraged her as much as his outstretched hand. He caught and steadied her and, when she recovered her breath and the tremor in her knees had stilled, she thanked him with a smile of her own. The trail was now less steep and she was able to divert her attention from the path to the steaming water coursing downhill beside her.

It chattered and babbled its way over moss-covered rocks and pooled in unexpected hollows beneath fallen trees or slapped up against slate-gray boulders. Ryan didn't hurry her as she stopped to investigate each mineral-encrusted pool. It intrigued her that so many varieties of mosses and weeds could survive in this alien environment, their finger-like multi-colored fronds waving gently in the constant current.

The trail wound its way down and joined a flight of steps that led to the entrance of the swimming pool area. The attendant on the gate greeted Ryan like an old friend and offered a friendly smile to Tilly as they entered. She stopped to watch the people in the pool, some swimming laps while others simply bobbed lazily around in groups just chatting. Sun-loungers lined the pool-side, many of them occupied by ladies wearing bathing suits, some of which seemed scandalously brief to her.

"Do you swim?" Ryan asked as he noted her interest.

"Not one of my accomplishments, I have to admit. What about you?"

"When you get thrown in a swimming hole, you have no choice," he said with a chuckle.

"Who would do such a thing?" Tilly stared at him, aghast.

"My brothers." Her indignation seemed to amuse him. "Josh was ten years old, Danny nine and I was just coming up to my seventh birthday. I guess they thought it was a practical present."

"But if you couldn't swim—"

"I learnt real fast. This way." Ryan entered the bathhouse and Tilly hurried to catch up with him. He stood by the darkened entrance to a tunnel where he stopped to wait for her.

"You'll need to watch your head a bit going through here." He slapped the hewn rock and the sound the flat of his hand made rang sharply in her ears. "This was dug out in 1886 to make it easier for visitors to see the cave."

Tilly followed him into the cavern. The sound of water overflowing from the pool and

68

rushing along the channel beside them drowned out the sound of her footsteps.

Once she was able to stand upright, the sight of the aquamarine-colored pool enchanted her. Sunlight streamed down through the vent high above her, illuminating the centre of the pool and making the clear water shimmer. Wisps of steam rose from its surface, their moist caress settling on her skin as gently as morning dew. For one fanciful moment, she imagined the pool to be breathing and knelt beside it, dipping her hand into the water and watching the resulting ripples radiate outward.

"It's as warm as a bath," she said, flicking droplets from her fingers.

"Which is why it's always been so popular," Ryan explained.

Tilly continued to gaze into the sparkling water, aware that Ryan waited patiently for her. When she got to her feet, he took her hand again and she made no protest as they walked back out into the sunshine.

"So if that was the cave," Tilly said, shading her eyes, "and this is the swimming pool and bathhouse, what is the basin?"

"I was saving it for last as we have to go past it to get out." Turning at the corner of the bathhouse, they came to a naturally formed bowl at the base of the rocks. "This is the original pool. It's not very deep, but it's warm and despite the smell supposed to be really relaxing."

Tilly pulled a face. "I'm not sure that I would want to bathe there and go home smelling of rotten eggs."

"Me neither." Ryan suddenly glanced upwards, scanning the still clear blue sky. A few cotton-wool clouds drifted overhead, but Tilly could see nothing to perturb her.

"What's wrong?"

Ryan grinned at her consternation. "Nothing. Just checking the time. It's going on four o'clock and I should be getting back to the barn."

"Oh, yes." Her years of living on the prairies had taught her the same skill. No need for a timepiece when all one had to do was measure the distance of shadows on the ground and check to see the position of the sun in the sky.

Boston seemed to be reluctant to stir himself from his afternoon doze. He shook his head, rattling his harness, as Ryan took up the reins and pointed him back down the road. Tilly could not believe that the day had passed so quickly, or that she had enjoyed Ryan's company so much. He was so different to the boys she remembered from back home. But then, she told herself, Ryan was no boy.

He was a strong, confident young man. She slid him a sideways glance. He appeared relaxed and happy, yet there was a maturity and strength in his face that impressed her. The more time she spent with him, the more she liked him.

Late afternoon sunshine streamed through the trees along the side of the road, dappling the surface with bars of light and shadow. Boston, head up and ears pricked now that he sensed he was going home, trotted along without any encouragement from his driver.

"You can drop me off at the bridge," Tilly said. "I'll walk from there."

"Are you sure?"

"Of course. It's my day off and you're supposed to be working. Will you get into trouble?"

Ryan shook his head. "Nope. All my chores at the barn were done before I picked up that delivery from the station. I just need to be there in case anyone is looking for an evening ride."

He pulled up just before the turn onto the bridge and Tilly jumped down from the wagon. She wanted to see him again but wasn't quite sure if she should ask him or just wait until he asked her. She didn't have to wait for long.

"On your next day off," he called as Boston took charge of their homeward trip, "I'll take you on a trail ride."

She waved him goodbye and laughed to herself as she set out along the path back to the hotel. In what she now recognized as Ryan's own confident way, he had told her what he was going to do.

Would he ever, she wondered, ask her what she wanted?

Chapter Nine

Tilly walked alongside the river, deep in thought. So much had happened to her that had not been of her choosing that she had never considered what she really did want. Now she had the time to think about herself, the effort of it pleated her brow into deep furrows.

Part of her heart yearned for her mother and her father and for the strength that came from their love and support. That strength was what she needed now. They had believed in and loved each other utterly, despite her mother's occasional grumbling, which was offset by her father's unruffled demeanor.

She half-smiled as she remembered the numerous times he had winked at her behind her mother's back. It was never done in a malicious way, more making them allies until her mother's usual good nature was restored. It never took long, especially if her father nuzzled her mother's neck, making her giggle and half-heartedly push him away.

If she truly wanted anything, Tilly realized, it was to have that kind of a relationship. Her position at the hotel was for here and now. It was no more than a stop-gap on the way to finding something more suitable and, if the afternoon with Ryan had made only one thing clear to her, it was that she needed to be outside.

Making beds, cleaning bathrooms, following the rigid but necessary housekeeping rules at the hotel, hemmed her in as much as the mountains did. Impressive though they were, she could not shake off the burning ache for the grand sweep of the prairies where she had grown up. In her mind's eye she saw again the long line of the endless horizon, an uninterrupted seam of land and sky.

She remembered a time when the rain had fallen and the sun shone in equal measure, creating the correct combination of heat and moisture to coax the crops out of the ground. There was no better sight, she thought, than that sea of breeze-rippled green, waving stalks, ebbing and flowing as did the tides. As the season progressed, so the green changed from the vibrant freshness of that first growth to the gold of ready-to-harvest grain.

But then everything changed. The sky was no longer blue but a brassy haze in which the sun hung like a burnished copper plate. The wind, when it came, was no longer gentle and cooling but stung like a hornet and bore in its passing every inch of the topsoil on which they depended. One year trailed into two, then three, repeating the droughts of the 1920's, which she barely remembered, and no one knew when it would end.

Being so deep in thought, she missed her turning to the hotel. Rather than go back, she continued on, drawn by the whisper and hiss of the river as it rushed along between its steep banks. She peeked between the branches, amazed at the speed at which the water raced past her. Contemplating the Bow Falls from the top floor of the hotel was a poor substitute for the reality of being beside it. Tons of water plunged through the hundred-foot gap between steep banks and cascaded down a thirty-foot drop in a froth of churning white water.

She stood at the river's edge, looking in wonder at all that water. She had never seen so much in her life nor had she imagined the sound of it. When someone touched her on the shoulder, she jumped and whirled about to find herself face to face with Burma Evans.

"You're the new girl, aren't you?" Burma wore a red plaid tam o'shanter with a matching scarf wrapped around her throat. She'd pulled her coat collar up to her ears and stuffed her hands into her pockets. She looked thoroughly miserable.

"Not quite so new now, Miss Evans." Tilly smiled at her a little nervously. Miss Richards had been very firm in her instructions about fraternizing with guests, although this encounter could hardly be deemed her fault. "I understand this is your second visit here?"

"Oh, that Fliss girl must have been talking." Burma shrugged. "One has to suppose that staff will chatter."

"Doesn't everyone?" Tilly put her hands into her own pockets. The sun was already sliding down the sky into evening and the bulk of the hillside behind them cast its shadow across the river. The dampness in the air began to chill her.

Burma shrugged again. "If one has someone to talk to, I suppose."

"But I thought you were here with your fiancée. Don't you talk to him?" Tilly blurted out the words before she considered what their impact may be.

"That was the plan, but I've hardly seen Frederic since we arrived." Burma kicked moodily at a pebble. Tilly's instincts told her the girl was deeply unhappy. "You see, he brought a couple of his friends with him, which was the last thing I expected. They're either off playing golf or going climbing and tonight, when I thought we might at least have dinner together, he'd arranged to play in a water-polo tournament. I watched it for a bit, but it's not really my idea of entertainment."

"But there must be several ladies that you could become friendly with."

"Yes, if I wanted to play tennis, or swim, or trail ride. I ask you, have you seen the nags they provide for that? I wouldn't give you a thank you for any one of them."

"Maybe," Tilly said slowly, remembering what Ryan had told her and considering her words carefully, "they are chosen for being the most suitable horses for the job."

"I should have insisted that I bring my own horses with me," Burma continued without giving any indication that she had heard Tilly. "My trainer says it is too long a trip for highly strung thoroughbreds, but at least I would be suitably mounted."

"Um, pardon me, but I understood that you live in New York City. Where can you keep horses there?"

Burma threw back her head and laughed out loud. "Oh, you ninny. I don't keep my horses there. We have a farm near Albany."

A long time had passed since Tilly sat with her father in their kitchen, poring over an atlas, both of them searching for answers to questions posed by her mother. After a moment of search her memory, she recalled certain maps and the place names dotted over them.

"That's in upstate New York, isn't it?"

One of Burma's elegant eyebrows crept upwards. "I'm surprised you knew that."

"Why?"

"Why what?"

The two girls glared at each other, one indignant and the other suddenly defensive.

"Why would it surprise you that I knew where Albany was?" Tilly demanded. "Do you think that because I am a chambermaid, I am uneducated and ignorant?"

"In my experience the two frequently go hand in hand."

"Oh, really? And just how many chambermaids do you actually know?" Tilly pulled her hands out of her pockets and fisted them on her hips.

"Well, now I come to think of it," Burma drawled, "I don't actually know any. Why would I?"

"Because it suits you not to know that these are people just like you except for their circumstances?" Tilly suggested. "They can be happy, they can bleed, they can be hurt when their boyfriends don't take them to dinner. Sound familiar?"

"My goodness, aren't you the little spitfire." Burma took a step back and looked Tilly up and down. "No one speaks to me like that. I shall have to report you to your supervisor."

The threat had the effect of cooling Tilly's temper, but only slightly. "Do what you like. I'm sure you always do."

Silence fell between the two of them and Tilly shivered. Arguing with Burma Evans had not been on her agenda, nor did she feel that an apology was in order. Burma had insulted her, not the other way around. Yet Burma had not rushed off in a high dudgeon at Tilly's outburst. Rather, she seemed not to want to leave and Tilly suddenly found herself feeling rather sorry for the girl.

"Do you want to stay here, or walk back up to the hotel with me?" she asked.

"Would you mind very much if I walked with you?" The tone in Burma's voice told Tilly that was as much of an apology as she was likely to get.

"Come on." Tilly clambered over some driftwood up to the pathway. "Why don't we stop into Sam's and have a coffee to get warm?"

"I'd like that." There was a note of relief in Burma's reply. "Can we start again?"

"Start what again?" Already striding up the hill, Tilly turned and looked back at Burma's disconsolate figure.

"Being friends?"

Tilly looked beyond the expensive clothes and the girl's finely drawn features. The world of hurt in Burma's anxious eyes touched her more deeply than she had been prepared for.

"On one condition," she said.

"Which is?"

That eyebrow lofted upwards again and Tilly decided it was a trick she would have to learn.

"Just be real with me," she said. "Don't put on airs and graces, don't take me for a fool, and I promise not to lose my temper with you again."

"My goodness, Tilly." Burma stared at her as if astonished. "If you think that was losing your temper, just wait until you see me lose mine."

Tilly couldn't help but laugh, yet beneath her apparent light heartedness there lurked an uncomfortable thought.

What if Burma did complain to Miss Richards? And if she did, what might the result of that complaint be?

Chapter Ten

Tilly brushed all her doubts aside as they walked into Sam's. The first person she spotted was Fliss, sitting with Saul and another bellhop whose name she didn't know. The look of astonishment that settled on Fliss' face when she saw Burma almost made Tilly laugh.

"Shall we join my friends, or would you prefer to sit at another table?" she asked, not sure if Burma would be offended by the invitation or even inclined to socialize with other members of staff from the hotel.

"Would they mind, do you think?" Burma almost looked wistful as she looked at the group.

In answer, Tilly smiled and led the way. She grabbed a spare chair from another table and set it down for Burma, then took her own seat, making sure that she could see both the bar and the door from where she sat. Ryan wasn't there but, if he did come in, she would not fail to see him.

She quickly made the introductions and learned that Jimmy Williams was as much a protégé to Saul as she was to Fliss. Jimmy had the advantage of having worked at The Palliser Hotel in Calgary and had decided, he said, to work his way out to the west coast as he had a hankering to see the ocean. Fliss remained unusually quiet while both Saul and Jimmy quickly became engaged in conversation with Burma about her traveling experiences. Her eyes began to sparkle with pleasure as she talked and Tilly sat back. Apart from her train trip from Medicine Hat, she had no similar experiences to share and simply listened while the chatter flowed over and around her.

Fliss nudged her surreptitiously and muttered, "Why did you bring her?"

It was a question that Tilly could not immediately answer because a familiar prickle at the back of her neck silenced her.

Frederic Vanderoosten had entered the bar and was walking towards them. His khaki-colored slacks, navy blazer and knotted silk cravat about his neck looked elegant and expensive. His hair, slicked back from his unlined forehead, shone with a liberal application of brilliantine. The popular style did nothing to conceal the look of arrogant indifference on his lean, clean-shaven face. His eyes narrowed as he came closer, changing his expression to one Tilly recognized as mean displeasure. As he came up beside Burma he placed his hand on her shoulder.

It could have been a friendly gesture of greeting, or it could have been a silent notice to Saul and Jimmy that Burma was spoken for. Either option should not have produced the flicker of pain in her eyes that made Tilly glance at Frederic's hand.

She saw immediately that his fingers had tightened their grip and knew that the pressure on Burma's shoulder, even through the protection her coat afforded, must be fierce.

"Hello, muffin." he drawled. "Slumming it, are we?"

He swept a scornful gaze over the group. No one spoke. Tilly glanced quickly to her right. Fliss picked at the edge of the table. Next to her, Jimmy gripped his long-neck more tightly. Across the table, Saul set his mouth in a tight line. To her dismay she found that her own mouth had turned to sawdust. She swallowed hard and looked directly at Frederic.

"Good evening, Mr. Vanderoosten," she said as calmly as she could. "Perhaps you would like to pull up a chair and join us?"

The shocked silence around her was broken, as she had hoped and prayed it would, by Frederic's burst of incredulous laughter.

"You may be a real cute patootie, but no thanks. I've bigger fish to fry." He gave Burma's shoulder a shake. "When you're ready to rise back up to your own level, I'll be over there with Jeremy."

Burma said nothing but simply nodded her head. When Frederic left them, she cast a nervous glance around the table, her face flushed with embarrassment.

"Will you believe that I am sorry for that?" she said softly.

Tilly reached over and gave her hand a sympathetic squeeze.

"Are you really going to marry that sap?" Fliss asked in a hard voice loaded with disbelief.

"Fliss," Tilly hissed. "That's none of your business."

Burma pushed her chair back and stood up. The hurt that Tilly had previously seen in her eyes hovered there again, but she smiled and thanked them for their company.

Saul got to his feet and said, "Anytime, Miss Evans."

Burma turned and walked away, not to join her fiancée and his friend, but to the door.

"Well," Fliss breathed. "What do you make of that?"

"All is not well in wonderland, that's for sure," Saul said as he sat down. "And you girls watch yourself if Vanderoosten's around. I wouldn't trust him an inch."

Although he spoke to both of them, Tilly was well aware that Saul had looked directly at Fliss as he issued his warning.

"So what's the scuttlebutt on this wedding?" Jimmy asked.

"Supposedly at the end of August." Fliss smiled and her eyes lit up at the prospect of the event. "They've invited two hundred guests. It's going to be a huge affair."

"Are they all staying at the Banff Springs?" Tilly pictured the hotel's walls bulging outwards and stifled a burst of amusement.

Fliss shrugged. "I suppose so. Burma's father has organized it all as far as I know, even down to ordering fresh caviar, shrimp cocktails, noisette of lamb Rossini, cold meats and salads and several desserts for the wedding luncheon."

"What the heck is noisette of lamb Rossini?" Jimmy scrunched up his nose and made a face.

"Noisette of lamb is a boneless lamb chop and the Rossini is a sauce made with spices, brandy and red wine," Saul explained.

"What's wrong with a plain 'ol lamb chop?" Jimmy asked.

"Never mind that," Fliss interrupted, "how did you know what this noisette thingy is, Saul?"

"I've always checked the menus wherever I've worked," Saul said with a grin. "Then if a guest asks what's good in the dining room I can give some sort of an answer rather than appear ignorant. The more you know about the hotels you work in, the more information you have to offer guests so the happier they will be with you. That often turns into a good tip. So take notice, young Jimmy."

His remark seemed to emulate Ryan's philosophy. A pang of loneliness lodged itself in her breast and Tilly realized that she had missed his company this evening. He had readily explained his absences as being due to taking out parties of horseback riders on the trails or overnight camping trips. On one occasion he had been gone for a whole week with a party of photographers. She wished that he had as regular a schedule as she did so that she could spend more time with him. When she finished her ruminations and looked up, both Saul and Fliss were eyeing her with amusement. "Where did your thoughts go rambling?" Saul asked her with a grin.

Fliss propped her elbows on the table, wove her fingers together and rested her chin on them. She fluttered her eyelashes and sighed, "Oh, Ryan."

Tilly knocked one of her elbows off the table and Fliss broke into a fit of giggles.

"Who's Ryan?" Jimmy asked.

"Tilly's boyfriend," Fliss told him as she went into another round of giggles.

"I don't know what's so funny." Tilly could not imagine what she had said or done to amuse them, for even Saul and Jimmy were grinning now.

"Your face." Fliss wiped away her tears of laughter. "Tilly, I swear I've never known anyone as easy to read as you. Whether you approve or disapprove, are happy or sad, it's as plain as a newspaper headline what you're thinking."

"All right. Tell me what I'm thinking now," Tilly challenged.

Fliss shook her head. "Not now you are in control of yourself. It's when you're not thinking that you show your thoughts."

"Well, she kept her thoughts to herself when she asked Vanderoosten to join us." Saul raised his glass to her. "I've never seen such a poker face. You shocked him, too, but better watch your back now, Tilly. He doesn't strike me as the forgiving type."

The same conclusion had occurred to her, and Tilly couldn't help thinking of what might come of it as she and Fliss walked back to their room. Nor could she stop thinking about Burma. Her first impressions of her had been of a spoilt but self-assured socialite. Now, having seen her literally in Frederic Vanderoosten's grip, Tilly brooded on the real nature of their relationship and couldn't shake off her persistent notion that something was wrong.

Fliss suddenly linked their arms and gave Tilly a shake. "All right, missy. Out with it. What's bothering you about Burma?"

"Oh, good Lord." Tilly rolled her eyes in exasperation. "It's just that...oh, I don't know, Fliss. Burma's just not as happy as a girl about to be married should be. I mean, look at it. Who wouldn't be happy getting married in a hotel like the Banff Springs? I can't imagine anything I would like better."

"But maybe," Fliss offered, "she didn't want to get married here. What if she wanted to get married in New York? What if she wanted to organize everything herself instead of having her father stage manage it? And what if Frederic is not the man she wants to marry?"

"That's an awful lot of 'what ifs', Fliss and," another thought struck Tilly, "have you noticed her wearing an engagement ring at all? I haven't."

"Maybe it's a hugely expensive pink diamond and stored in the hotel safe." Fliss yawned. "I don't know, Tilly, and to be honest with you, I really don't care."

Tilly couldn't blame her. She had her own problems to contend with, and nothing either of them could say or do would likely help Burma.

Despite the unresolved problems rattling around in her mind Tilly found that, once she settled down in bed, her thoughts returned to the time she had spent that day with Ryan.

She had enjoyed it so much. His easy smile and the twinkle in his eye when he looked at her made her feel special. His interest and enthusiasm for the people and events that had contributed to Banff's growth wasn't just to impress visitors, it was very real to him. Most of all she liked that she could trust him.

A smile played across her mouth as she drifted into sleep. She was more than half way to loving him but she would not be taken for granted.

If Ryan Blake wanted her to be his wife, he would have to ask her to marry him.

Chapter Eleven

Tilly fixed her cap and smoothed her apron before pushing the service cart out into the hall. She hummed softly as she started her day. Yesterday evening Miss Burma Evans had shown a softer, more vulnerable side, one that Tilly had never suspected might exist. The thought that something was very wrong still troubled her as she knocked on Burma's door.

"Housekeeping, Miss Evans," she called, and waited.

A sound, as if something had fallen, or been pushed over, came faintly through the door. Tilly checked the door handle. No 'Do Not Disturb' notice had been hung there. She knocked again.

"In." The short instruction to enter gave her an indication of Burma's mood this morning.

She quickly selected the linens and towels she required, opened the door and walked in but faltered when she set eyes on the occupant.

Burma, swathed in her scarlet robe, had her hair tucked up into a matching turban. From the diamante pin clipped to its centre point a feather, matching those trimming the robe, swept back over her head. The effect was decidedly dramatic, but it was the large dark glasses covering half of her face that captured Tilly's attention.

"Do not say a word," Burma instructed in a voice so brittle Tilly expected the words to shatter into tiny pieces on the floor.

"O-of course not," she stammered and hurried into the bedroom.

All her fears concerning the other girl came flooding back as she went to the bed. The pillows were in a haphazard heap against the headboard. The turquoise comforter and rumpled sheets trailed in a tangled mess onto the floor. The stale smell of cigarette smoke made her wrinkle her nose and drew her attention to the ashtray, full to overflowing, on the nightstand. She frowned. She knew Burma favored Lucky Strikes, which she smoked infrequently and always fitted into an elegant cigarette holder. The debris in the ashtray contained two different brands of cigarettes, with no cigarette holder in sight.

Tilly stripped the bed and quickly remade it. It was no concern of hers what might have occurred here last night, and yet she still could not shake the feeling that Burma was in real trouble. She hurried through cleaning the rest of the suite while Burma stared moodily out of the window.

"Is there anything else, Miss Evans?" Tilly asked when she had done.

"No, thank you." Burma did not look at her.

Tilly gathered up the soiled linens and damp towels she had removed from the bathroom, but before she reached the door Burma stopped her.

"I want to make one thing clear, McCormack." Tilly looked up in surprise at the harsh tone that might have come from Miss Richards's own mouth, not Burma's. "The socializing of yesterday evening will not be repeated, and you and I are not friends."

"Of course not, Miss Evans," Tilly assured her. "If there's nothing else, I'll wish you a good morning."

Tilly frowned as she closed the door behind her. She knew Burma could be rude and impetuous and, after observing her closely since starting to work at the hotel, concluded that this was more of a front than the girl's true personality. Either there was a decent person struggling to break out, or Burma was afraid. Of what or of whom should not concern her, but it did. There had been bruises on Burma's neck and, despite her attempt to hide them beneath the collar of her feathered robe, Tilly had not missed them.

"What do you think I should do?" she asked Fliss later as they sat together at lunchtime.

"Nothing." Fliss sighed. "Look, Tilly, it's great that you care, that's just who you are. But we are not allowed to get involved with the guests here. We are polite and helpful to them and pass the time of day when we see them, but that's it. Anything else is not for the likes of us."

"But—"

"But nothing, Tilly," Fliss snapped in frustration. "Just let it go before Miss Richards lets you go, because that's what it will come to if you carry on with this. Burma Evans is only one of over five hundred guests here right now, so drop it."

Tilly set off with her cart to clean the rest of her allocation of rooms. As she stripped beds, folded and tucked sheets and fluffed up pillows, she could not shake the picture of the bruises around Burma's neck from her mind. She could not have done that to herself and there were the two brands of cigarettes in the ashtray, which made her, think that Burma had had company last night. Was it Frederic Vanderoosten?

She didn't want to argue with Fliss, nor could she ignore the depth of her own convictions. By the time she finished her shift she had reached a decision. Her common sense told her she was taking a risk, but she remembered how her father, if he found a critter in trouble, either put it out of its misery or fixed it. The first choice was not an option, but if she could help Burma, she would.

When she stowed her service cart, she picked up two clean ashtrays and a dusting cloth. If anyone asked why she was still there, better to be ready with a plausible excuse. She paused at the junction of all the corridors, but there was no one about. The whole floor could have been abandoned. She turned into Burma's wing and marched along to her suite where she stopped and looked over her shoulder. There was still no one about, so she took a deep breath and steeled herself before she knocked on the door.

There was no response but she was sure that Burma was still inside. She knocked again and waited. Just as she decided that no one could be there, soft footfalls approached the door. She was sure it was Burma. Time stopped in the drowsy afternoon and, just as she was about to turn away, she heard a sound that could have been a sob.

"Go away, Freddy." Burma's voice was choked with tears. "I told you I don't want to see you."

Anger raged through Tilly as she realized who had caused Burma's bruises, but she calmed herself. Allowing that anger to cloud her judgement would do no one any good.

"It's me, Miss Evans," she said. "May I come in?"

Tilly waited for what seemed an eternity but in reality could only have been a few seconds at most. Burma had been so abrupt earlier that day. Maybe she really had meant what she had said, but Tilly almost didn't care. The girl had seemed so hurt and, in spite of her harsh words, strangely defenceless. Tilly could no more let it go than she could leave a wounded animal.

After a moment more of silence the key clicked in the lock, the handle turned and the door opened a little. The wedge of space it offered was wide enough for Tilly to quickly step inside. The drapes were half-closed but there was enough light for her to see items of clothing littering the floor, as if Burma had started to get dressed in one outfit then changed her mind. Various pieces of delicate pastel colored underwear looked like a shower of flower petals amidst dresses and shoes.

Shocked, she looked at Burma, hoping for some indication of the reason for the wreckage. All she received was a sardonic shrug and the trade-mark raised eyebrow before Burma threw herself nonchalantly onto the sofa. Her apparent lack of concern was a poor front for the fact that she was deeply hurt and trying not to show it. Tilly folded herself into the chair closest to the sofa.

"I know it's none of my business," she said, keeping her voice as calm as she could, "and I'm sorry if I'm speaking out of turn, but why did he do it?"

"Because...." Burma's eyes brimmed with tears and she brushed them away with the back of her hand while she tried to control herself.

"Here." Tilly offered her the dusting cloth. "Get it out of your system. I won't tell anyone, and I'm not going anywhere until you feel more like yourself."

After a few sobs and hiccups and a lot of sniffs, Burma began to relax.

"Thank you, Saint Tilly," she said with a final sniff. "You know you are too good to me, don't you? Especially after the way I snapped at you this morning. I'm sorry."

"Don't concern yourself about that. I knew something was wrong even before I saw the bruises on your neck."

Burma unconsciously reached up and massaged her neckline. "These aren't quite so bad. At least I can cover them with a scarf"

"Are you really going to marry a man who could do this to you?" Tilly asked.

Burma picked at the piping that trimmed the arm of the sofa and shook her head. "I found out some things about Freddy that are totally unsupportable. When I confronted him, he didn't deny any of it, so I broke off the engagement. There will be no wedding. Freddy was so furious he just grabbed me around the neck and shook me. This is the result."

Tilly thought back to her first night in Sam's bar. The way Frederic Vanderoosten had looked at her had made her skin crawl, and Fliss had not been at all complimentary about him either.

Burma got to her feet and strode restlessly about the room. "It seems he thought he would get his hands on a lot of money once we were married. The money was the attraction, not me. When I told him that I don't have control of my funds and only receive a small monthly allowance, he lost it. I mean, he really was livid. Oh, I wish I was dirt poor."

Tilly hissed in a breath. She could not trust herself to speak, so stood up and went to the closest heap of clothes. Picking up a pair of French knickers, the rose-pink satin edged with delicate cream-colored lace, she ran her fingers over the smooth fabric before folding them and placing them on the chair she had just vacated.

"No, you don't," she said when she found her voice again. "You wouldn't enjoy being dirt poor at all. It would mean you never knew what it was like to wear lingerie like this. It would mean you getting up about the time you usually arrive home in the morning."

She picked up the matching camisole and folded it, too.

"In summer you would stumble out of bed into the pre-dawn to check the stock and milk the cows. When dawn broke, you would have enough light to see to collect the eggs and at sunrise, you would be making breakfast and getting as much done as you could before it got too hot to work. And in winter…, well, I bet you've never had to run a rope from your front deck to the barn so you wouldn't lose your way in a blizzard, or gone out to break the ice on the water troughs, or eaten oatmeal for days because your pantry was almost bare. There would be no champagne and canapés, no fancy clothes, just clothes that would, if you were lucky, mostly keep you warm."

Burma slowly sat up, her eyes widening. "Were things really that bad for you?"

"Yes. At times, they were." Tilly set the folded camisole on top of the knickers. "So don't talk that nonsense about being poor to me. Tell me about Freddy instead. I thought he was quite wealthy."

"As did everyone else." Burma slumped back onto the sofa. "I did too. We met here last year and had a wonderful time together. When we went back to New York we kept bumping into each other at parties and dinners and continued to see each other. We got engaged at Christmas and it was Freddy's idea for us to get married here, where we first met. I thought it all so romantic. I mean, who wouldn't?"

Not knowing what to say, Tilly kept quiet.

"Once the ring was on my finger, Freddy began to change." For a moment Burma's voice quavered and she bit her lip. "It was subtle at first. Little things, but always about money."

"And then you started arguing?"

"Bitterly and frequently." Burma took another turn around the room, chewing on the side of her finger. "And Papa was no help. According to him he'd spent vast amounts of money on my education and expected to me to pay attention to my fiancée as I'd been trained to do."

"What did he mean by that?" Tilly picked up and folded more clothes.

"After boarding school, I was packed off to finishing school in Lausanne. I really liked it there. All those lovely, narrow streets where the houses crowd in on each other and you wander for hours until you suddenly find yourself in a quaint, cobbled square with a Gothic church at one end and a cafe at the other. But the whole point of finishing school is to learn social etiquette and how to behave in society. One must not let one's life partner down over the lobster bisque."

Burma pulled a face as Tilly burst out laughing. "You may well laugh, but it truly was a lesson. Maybe not in those exact words, but that was the core of it. You see, the whole point of finishing school is to learn how to attract a husband, preferably a wealthy one, and support all his endeavours. And, because Freddy and I were now engaged, Papa expected me to do as my husband-to-be told me."

Tilly couldn't imagine anything less romantic. "That sounds perfectly dreadful."

"Oh, wait, it gets worse." Burma started pacing again. "At Easter, one of my girlfriends swore she'd seen Freddy with another woman." Tilly refrained from repeating what Fliss had told her. "He denied it, of course, and was as sweet and loving as he'd been last year, but then he started to hurry our wedding plans along. Instead of discussing it with me, he took it all to Papa and they arranged everything together. The only thing I insisted on, and managed to get my way with, was my wedding gown."

"Is it here?"

Burma shook her head. "That is coming with Papa and the rest of the wedding paraphernalia."

"You haven't told him yet?" Tilly couldn't help but wonder how Mr. Evans would take the news.

"Every time I've picked up the phone I haven't gone as far as putting the call through," Burma admitted. "Papa really likes Freddy and I'm not sure if he'll believe me. I don't exactly have a brilliant relationship with my father. Did you get on with yours?"

Burma's question took Tilly by surprise.

"Yes, I did," she said slowly, and after giving the question some thought, added, "In fact, we got on very well. Although, when he was alive, I never thought about it much."

"When did he die?"

Tilly took a breath and briefly closed her eyes. The pain of losing him was still too fresh and a lump rose in her throat as she whispered, "February."

"What happened to the farm?"

"The bank foreclosed. They had to." Tilly shrugged in resignation. "That's why I'm here."

"Oh, Tilly. I'm so sorry." Burma patted the sofa beside her. "Come and sit down and tell me about it."

Tilly hesitated and then sat down. She wasn't sure why she felt so drawn to Burma. They were as far apart on the social scale as they could possibly be and yet she felt closer to her than Fliss. She considered their differences and decided it could only be that she more understood Burma's vulnerability than Fliss' in-the-moment flippancy.

"Was it very bad?" Burma asked, bringing Tilly back to the present.

"At times it was dreadful," Tilly said with a sigh. "At least our well never quite ran dry and I kept chickens and carried on working Mom's garden, so we had vegetables which a neighbour taught me how to can. At least we could keep food on the table."

"How old were you when your mom died?"

Tilly looked away and held on to the stab of pain that thinking of her mother produced. "I was seven."

"Seven?" Burma's eyes opened wide in shock. "Seven years old and you were growing a garden? Couldn't your father have done that?"

"Not with everything else that had to be done."

"What about school?"

"Oh, I mostly went to school." Tilly smiled. "On days that I didn't, Dad would sit down at the kitchen table with me in the evening after supper and we'd talk about history or geography or whatever we were working on in school, and he always made sure I had plenty of books to read."

"My mother left us when I was ten," Burma confided, "but I didn't have to do anything. We had a chef and a housekeeper and maids. I had a nanny up until my mother left and then Papa sent me to boarding school."

"Did you like that?"

Burma pulled a face. "Not really. The teachers were very strict and didn't much like me. I wasn't a gracious pupil, you see. They were glad to see the back of me when I was old enough to go to finishing school. Switzerland was more fun anyway, especially when we were allowed out and met up with some of the local people. It gave us an opportunity to practise our social skills."

"I can't imagine what it must be like to travel to another country." Tilly looked beyond the mountains outside the window and let her imagination run riot with visions of Balinese temples, grand palaces, and steaming jungles.

"It depends which country as to whether it's fun or not."

Tilly pulled herself out of her daydreaming and stared at Burma. "How many countries have you travelled to?"

Burma thought for a moment. "Well, after Switzerland, Papa took me on something of a Grand Tour through Europe. Papa, of course, was more interested in the railway systems in each country rather than the scenery. Damn railways. He wouldn't even come to Sundance Canyon with me last year because there wasn't train service there. He tried to make it a joke and I know I was lucky to have done all that travelling, so I didn't really mind, but I should still like to go there."

Tilly couldn't imagine where she would go first if all her expenses were paid and laughed at the idea. "Coming to Banff is the furthest I've ever been," she admitted, "and I don't know that I will ever go anywhere else."

"What, you won't go south with the rest of the staff when the season ends?"

Tilly shook her head. "Not likely. I think I'll stay in Banff and see what work I can pick up until the hotel reopens next year. And, if I don't get back to work now, I might not have a job to come back to."

She got to her feet and smoothed out the wrinkles in her apron, hoping that no one had been looking for her.

"Thanks for talking to me," Burma said softly.

"I enjoyed your company," Tilly answered honestly as she walked to the door. She hesitated before she added, "Take care of those bruises. If you want anything, let me know. I'll see you in the morning."

Tilly let herself out and closed the door quietly. Had she done the right thing in offering aid to Burma? She knew the hotel management, while demanding that guests' every need and whim was satisfied, did not approve of the staff forming friendships with them. It was too late for that now.

She took care of the ashtrays and dusting cloth and decided to use the stairs instead of the elevator. As she reached the first landing a prickle of awareness across the back of her neck made her stop. It was not the same as the sensation that Frederic Vanderoosten's presence raised in her, but she looked back up the stairs just to be sure that he was not there.

The stair well was empty except, yet it seemed to shimmer and vibrate with an unseen energy. The lights dimmed, as if winking at her then returned to full power. She tried to take another step but found she could not move. Her breathing became ragged and heavy as ice-cold, unseen hands took hers and drew her towards the stairs. She wanted to scream but couldn't. Panic rose in her. Her vision blurred and faded to black.

Chapter Twelve

Someone was patting her cheek. She swatted the hand away. It wasn't time to get up. It couldn't be for she had only just gone to sleep. The bed seemed more uncomfortable than usual so she turned and settled more comfortably on her side.

There was that dratted hand again. Couldn't she be left alone?

"Tilly! Tilly, wake up." Now somebody was shaking her.

Gradually her senses returned and she slowly opened her eyes to see Fliss crouched beside her.

"What's wrong?" she mumbled, blinking sleepily up at Fliss.

"You tell me." Fliss managed to get her arm behind Tilly's back and hauled her into a sitting position. "If a guest had found you they would have thought you were dead drunk. How long have you been here?"

Tilly covered her face with her hands and shook her head. "I have no idea."

"But what happened? Did you fall?" Fliss helped her to her feet. Tilly swayed a little and grabbed the banister rail for support.

Fliss frowned at her and sniffed her breath. "Are you sure you haven't been drinking?"

"Yes, I'm sure." Tilly pushed her away. "Just let me catch my breath a minute."

When her pulse returned to normal, Tilly took a deep breath and blew it out slowly between her pursed lips. "Well, that was odd."

"Odd?" Fliss fell into step beside her as Tilly started down the stairs. "How do you mean, odd?"

Tilly opened her mouth and then closed it again. What could she say that would make any sense of what she had experienced?

"Maybe I'm just a bit overwrought from dealing with Burma," she offered.

"Not to the extent for you to be found sleeping like a baby in the middle of that landing, you aren't," Fliss snorted. "And when I spoke to Burma she said you were fine."

"You spoke to her?" Tilly almost missed a step in surprise at Fliss' admission.

"When I couldn't find you, I suspected you might have gone to see her after all so I telephoned to her room." Fliss lifted a shoulder in an offhand shrug.

"Well, thank you for that." Tilly thought of all the warnings Fliss had given her. "That couldn't have been easy for you."

"It wasn't, and I probably wouldn't have bothered if it hadn't been for Ryan coming to look for you."

A little bump in her heart put a spring into Tilly's step as they walked outside. She hadn't given him a thought since this morning. Now, knowing that she'd missed seeing him gave her

103

a physical ache. "Did he say where he'd be tonight?"

"He said he'd try to get to Sam's later. I suppose we should go because I'm guessing you haven't eaten anything since lunchtime."

She hadn't even thought about food and wasn't even sure that she wanted anything, but Tilly washed up and tidied her hair anyway. Pulling the comb through her curls gave her time to consider what had happened to her that afternoon. There was nothing concrete, nothing she could put her finger on and say it was this or it was that. All she could remember was the shifting light and those ice-cold hands on hers.

That had to be her imagination. It couldn't have been anything else. Yet something niggled at the edges of her mind, elusive but there. She tapped the end of the comb against her bottom lip as she concentrated on the wayward thought. It had something to do with Fliss, she was sure of it but nothing surfaced. She sighed. If she stopped trying to recall what it was, maybe it would come to her of its own accord.

A rap on the bathroom door brought her to her senses and she hurriedly finished tidying up.

"You certainly took your time," Fliss said as they walked out into the evening sunshine. "You still look as pale as a ghost though."

Ghost. The thought that had eluded her finally surfaced. It was the expression she had seen on Fliss' face that first night when she had been telling them the story of the Ghost Bride. She hadn't really wanted to tell it at all, Tilly

104

thought now. The words had tumbled out as quickly as Fliss could form them and she had finished with, "End of story", as if she wanted nothing more to do with it. Tilly recalled Fliss' tight features and the way she pressed her lips together in a tight line. Saul had butted in then and made a joke of it and the moment had passed.

Tilly slowed her pace and caught Fliss' arm. "You've seen her, haven't you?"

"Seen who?" A wary look crept into Fliss' eyes but Tilly's grip on her arm prevented her from hurrying on.

"The Ghost Bride," Tilly said. "You've seen her."

Fliss shook off her hand and started forward again. "That's only a silly story. Who'd believe a thing like that?"

"You do," Tilly persisted. "I know it. And I saw her today too. Well, at least felt something."

"You must have been feeling faint when you started down those stairs," Fliss scoffed.

Tilly caught her arm again and spun her around. "Fliss, I felt perfectly fine when I started down stairs. No light-headedness, no weak knees or nausea. The air just changed. It felt charged like when there's a thunderstorm blowing in and then I had a prickling sensation at the back of my neck similar to when Frederic's around. But he wasn't there. Then the lights flickered and something took hold of my hands."

Tilly held out her hands, as if looking at them now could conjure up a firm impression of the sensation that cold grip had left her with.

"You were imagining things, Tilly." Fliss now looked stubborn. "That story must have been in your subconscious and you just happened to recall it as you were coming down stairs."

"No." Tilly shook her head, her own stubborn streak beginning to surface. "When Saul continued on with the story, he said, 'And some of the staff will tell you the same'. He meant you, didn't he?"

Fliss puffed out her cheeks and anger sparked in her eyes. "He had no business saying that and you're too sharp for your own good, but all right, yes, I did see something. Satisfied now?"

"I knew it." The admission delighted Tilly. "Now tell me the rest of it."

They had reached the horse corral. Fliss stopped and rested her arms along the top rail, staring across the dusty arena as if uncertain of what to say. "I've seen her twice now, once in the ballroom and then at the top of the stairs where she was supposed to have fallen."

"You didn't feel her? She didn't touch you?" Tilly asked.

Fliss shook her head. "Nope. She was just there, or maybe she wasn't. How should I know? It could have all just been my imagination as I'm sure it was yours."

Tilly shook her head. "I don't believe it was and I don't believe you've told me everything. Come on, Fliss. It's not like I'm not going to believe you after my own experience."

"Oh, good Lord," Fliss huffed. "Are you practising to be a nagging wife?"

"I'll give up when you do," Tilly promised.

Fliss sighed. "Alright. When I was in the ballroom I thought I saw a shadow passing across the floor. It came closer and I looked up, not sure what could have made it. And then I saw her. She was dancing and looked so happy. She smiled at me and then she was gone."

"And the next time?"

"I was going up the stairs and she just appeared at the top of the flight." Fliss closed her eyes and swallowed hard. "She held up a gold ring threaded onto a chain, smiled at me and said, "I know"."

Both girls fell silent. A hopeful crow settled on the fence a little way from them. When no reward for its bobbing and weaving performance was forthcoming, it flew off with raucous complaint into the tops of the trees on the far side of the corral.

"Not a figment of your imagination then," Tilly said quietly.

Fliss turned her head. "No, I don't think so. When I told Saul he thought maybe it was a result of my guilty conscience."

"But you've got nothing to be guilty about." The brief expression of hurt and defeat that Tilly saw in Fliss' eyes caught her by surprise.

"No?" Fliss shrugged and sighed. "Well, maybe not, but I would so love to wear my ring on my finger and not have to hide it. The only time we do wear our rings is when Saul and I are alone together. It somehow makes us closer."

"Are you sure there's nothing else you and Saul could do?" Tilly asked.

"Oh, come on, Tilly." Fliss straightened up. "You know what it's like right now. If Saul left this job he'd likely finish up in one of those government work camps for single, unemployed men and they're treated no better than slave labor. They work on roads, in construction and whatever else is needed all for twenty cents a day. No one can live on that."

Tilly nodded. "Yes, and I read about the On-to-Ottawa unemployment march that left Calgary in June. They only got as far as Regina where the whole thing finished in riots. The police tried to blame it on the marchers, but by all accounts it was the police action that caused all the rioting. I suppose we are really lucky to be here."

A line of trail riders emerged from between the trees, catching their attention. They fell silent as the horses shuffled into the corral, heading for their own spot against the fence.

"Can you imagine what it must be like to have enough money to come and stay here, to afford to go riding and tour around sight-seeing?

I wonder if they know how lucky they are."
Fliss sounded quite envious.

Tilly breathed in the tang of leather and strong aroma of the horses. Several cowboys came forward to help riders dismount but one rider in particular caught her eye. Happiness flooded through her, warming her cheeks and bringing a smile of pleasure to her lips. Ryan stepped down from the big, blue roan horse he rode, looked her way and sent her a brief nod before helping some of the riders.

"I'm going on in," Fliss said. "Are you coming or will you wait for him?"

"No, I'll come. He still has to deal with the horses and will be awhile yet."

Tilly pushed off the fence, tingling with awareness. She smiled at Ryan as she passed him and caught his answering smile. Neither spoke but she knew with certainty that he would be with her as soon as he could. A sudden thought struck her that, in some unhurried and inevitable way, they were being drawn together, much as the icy hands had drawn her down the stairs.

"Fliss," she gasped. "What time did Ryan come looking for me?"

Fliss frowned. "I don't know for sure, but it must have been about four or four-thirty. Somewhere around there. Why?"

Her mind whirling, Tilly quickly calculated what time she had left Burma. "That must have been it," she muttered. "That was why I felt as though I was being pulled down the stairs. The

Ghost Bride knew Ryan was looking for me and was trying to hurry me along."

The look Fliss gave her almost made Tilly take a step back. "Now that is your imagination working overtime," Fliss said in disgust. "For goodness' sake, Tilly, don't go spreading that tale around or people will think you're crazy."

The more she thought about it, she knew she wasn't crazy. She knew exactly what she had felt and considered it a reasonable conclusion that a bride who had not been able to fulfill her destiny might help others achieve theirs.

She said no more as she and Fliss found seats and ordered supper. By the time they had eaten Saul had joined them and shortly after that, Ryan came in.

"Where were you today?" he asked as he sat down beside her.

Tilly turned to face him. "One day I might tell you. But not today because I want to hear what you've been doing."

She placed her elbow on the table and rested her chin on the heel of her hand. She let her fingers curl up over the curve of her cheek. She smiled and fluttered her eyelashes a little.

"Why, Miss McCormack," Ryan said softly, "I do believe you are flirting with me."

The noise around her in the bar drifted away as she gazed into Ryan's eyes. "Yes, I think I am. How am I doing so far?"

"Not bad, not bad at all." He took her hand and entwined his fingers with hers. It seemed to her to be the most natural thing in the world. "It tells me you are beginning to like me a bit."

"More than a bit," she whispered. She looked at the fullness of his lower lip, the bow of his upper and the creases that formed at the corners of his mouth as he smiled at her. What would that mouth feel like on hers? And did he want to find out as badly as she did?

Chapter Thirteen

"Well, well, well."

The lazy drawl made Tilly look up and she froze as Frederic's hard, pewter-gray gaze settled on her. She tightened her grip on Ryan's hand and fought to keep her breathing even. How had he managed to approach without her inbuilt alarm system sounding the alarm? Ryan, she thought. Her awareness of him had made her unaware of anything else.

Ryan pushed his chair back and stood up. "Evenin', Mr. Vanderoosten," he said politely. "Anything I can help you with, sir?"

Tilly glanced at both of them. Ryan, not as tall as Frederic but more solidly built, and Frederic, tall and slim, his fine features drawn into a sardonic sneer. He flicked a mean glance at Tilly and the sneer changed into a thin smile.

"I was hoping to have taken up Miss McCormack's offer of her company, but it seems I have missed my chance. Another time, perhaps."

He wandered off towards the bar and, as Ryan slowly took his seat, Tilly released the breath she held.

"What was that all about?" He spoke quietly, but tension edged his eyes.

Before she could speak, Saul quickly explained what had happened the evening Burma had joined them.

"And," Fliss added for emphasis, "Tilly didn't invite him to join her, she invited him to join us, as a group. He's obviously chosen to misinterpret what she said."

Ryan took Tilly's hand again and gave it a little shake. "Just watch out for him, Tilly. He's as mean as a rattlesnake and will strike twice as fast if you give him the chance."

Tilly nodded. "Fliss warned me, and I've already seen the results of his temper."

Instantly she wanted to bite her tongue. She had promised Burma she would say nothing and yet here she was almost on the point of divulging that confidence. In answer to the questions she now found herself bombarded with from Saul and Fliss, she simply shook her head.

"I promised I wouldn't say anything, and I won't," she insisted.

"That's okay," Ryan comforted her. "We don't expect you to. But if anything gets out of hand, anything at all, make sure you tell one of us. Promise?"

Tilly nodded, suddenly overwhelmed as she realized how much these people meant to her now. Ryan and Saul suddenly got up in unison, as if they had sent each other a silent signal, and went to the bar. Watching them go, uneasiness gnawed at Tilly's heart. Frederic had already vanished so she was sure they were not about to confront him. They seemed to be chatting easily enough, joking with the barman and a couple of packers who had come in. She continued to watch them thoughtfully.

"What do you think they are up to?" she asked Fliss.

"Priming the community," Fliss answered dryly. "I don't think Frederic will find it so easy this year to cause the same sort of havoc as last. The packers will likely do what they can to keep an eye on him when he's out and about, and I know Saul has already talked to the bellhops at the hotel."

"Isn't there anyone there that we can tell?"

Fliss shook her head. "Nope. He's there on Mr. Evans's dime and plays that card as much as he can. If he had to pay his own bill, well, he'd either not be here in the first place, or kicked out, because I know for a fact he wouldn't be able to pay it. The man's a leech. Why do you think he made a play for Burma in the first place?"

"You knew he was after the money he thought she had?"

"Of course. Everyone did." Fliss settled back in her chair, but she kept her eyes fixed on Saul's back. "Everyone gossips in a hotel whether they are supposed to or not. So, last year, it was no secret that Mr. Evans had set Burma up for the season with a $60,000 letter of credit. Frederic had taken no notice of her until he caught wind of that and then he hardly left her side."

"Poor Burma," Tilly murmured.

"Oh, yes. Poor girl, with all Daddy's moola to draw on." Fliss stubbed out the cigarette she'd been smoking with short, stabbing strokes. "I was lucky if I got a dime from my dad and goodness knows what kind of a pickle he and Mom are in now."

"You don't keep in touch with them?" Tilly was sure that if her parents were still alive she would want to write letters to them.

"I sent a postcard from Miami at Christmas but really, Saul and I move around so much I never think of it."

Ryan and Saul sauntered back to them then, but Tilly could tell from the expressions on their faces something had changed. An air of collusion hovered between them which Tilly had no intention of questioning, knowing that somehow it concerned her and Fliss' safety and she was grateful for it.

They took a slow walk back, Saul and Fliss a little ahead and deep in conversation. Ryan walked more and more slowly until he stopped altogether and turned Tilly to face him.

"You do know what you started this evening, don't you?" he asked.

"I think so." Tilly looked at his mouth and her own ran dry. Her heart thudded painfully but she liked that Ryan was the cause. He drew her into the shadow of the trees and put his arms around her. With a sigh she rested her head on his chest. It felt so right.

"I don't have much to offer right now, Tilly," he said above her head. "I've got a good horse and a not-so-good dog and I bunk with the boys, but I've got my eye on a cabin which might be available next spring. Think you can wait 'til then?"

Tilly tightened her arms around him and breathed in the scent of him. Did she dare flirt more? She looked up at him and whispered, "Only if you kiss me now."

He lowered his head to hers. Tilly took a breath and closed her eyes. She had only been kissed once, a quick, sloppy buss on the mouth she knew to have been the result of a dare. She had quickly dismissed it, but this was different. Every part of her tingled with anticipation. When their lips met in one soft, sweet moment of tenderly giving and taking, she fell all the way in love.

They stood together in the darkness with the distant sound of rushing water vying with the rustle of leaves in the gentle breeze around them. Somewhere close by an owl hooted and they reluctantly broke apart. Tilly lifted her fingers to Ryan's mouth, reading the contours and texture of his lips. She felt him smile and saw that same smile soften his eyes. He leaned in and kissed her again.

"Come on," he said when he finally released her. "I'll walk you back to your door."

They talked quietly as they walked, their conversation broken by occasional laughter as they shared a joke or teased one another.

It was, Tilly thought, the most wonderful evening of her life. Just before Ryan left her, he chucked her on the chin and she smiled up at him.

"I'll see you tomorrow," he said. "Wear pants if you've got them. I'm taking you trail riding."

Tilly almost groaned. There it was again, that proprietary streak that gave Ryan his take-charge attitude. It might work for guides and packers, but it sure wasn't going to work for her. She fisted her hands on her hips.

"I'm going to marry you. I'm going to take you riding," she stormed. "Doesn't it ever cross your mind that a girl might like to be asked what she wants?"

Ryan looked at her in mild astonishment. "Don't you want to go riding?"

"That's not the point," Tilly sputtered. "Why can't you just ask me, instead of tell me? I do have an opinion of my own you know."

An easy-going shrug of his shoulder infuriated her more. "All right. Would you like to go trail riding with me tomorrow?"

"Thank you." Tilly tilted her chin up as she glared at him. "I would very much like to go riding with you and I do have pants and boots."

"Hmm." He appeared to be considering her response. The gleam of humor in his eyes put her on edge and she looked up at him warily, waiting for the comeback she knew would come.

"So, if you're coming with me anyway," he said, "why make all that fuss? Why not just say okay?"

"Because you can't just take it for granted that I'll fall in with your plans," Tilly stormed. "What if I'd wanted to do something else?"

"Do you?"

"Ryan!" She threw up her hands in despair. "I can see that arguing with you will be like trying to catch a cloud."

"Don't waste your time then." He kissed the tip of her nose, wished her goodnight, and walked off leaving her laughing.

"Someone's happy," Fliss commented as Tilly let herself into their room.

"Yes, I am." She hung up her jacket and kicked off her shoes. "Tomorrow just can't come fast enough."

"Better switch that light off then." Fliss already had her head down and Tilly quickly followed suit.

Chapter Fourteen

Tilly's work had become a smooth routine and her day was done almost before she knew it. It took her no time at all to race back to her room and change into a pair of corduroy pants and her boots. Her fingers trembled with anticipation as she laced them up and hurried to the corral where Ryan had said he would wait for her.

As soon as she turned the corner of the hotel she saw his roan horse and, tethered beside it, a white, sleepy looking pony. Two young women were making a fuss of the horses and flirting with Ryan. An unexpected jolt of hot, fierce jealousy bloomed in her chest, but it gave her a tug of satisfaction to see their faces fall when he smiled at her. There was no doubt where his interest lay and he tipped his hat to the ladies as he walked towards her. Her confidence rose and she welcomed him with a beaming smile.

"All ready to saddle up?" His pleasure at seeing her showed in the way his eyes crinkled at the corners as he returned her smile.

Tilly peeped around him at the white pony. Its saddle sat on the corral fence.

"Actually," she said slowly, "I've never saddled a horse."

"But you said you rode your mules." Ryan looked a little confused.

"Yes, but I didn't have a saddle," Tilly admitted. "I always rode bareback."

"All right then." He nodded that he understood. "So let's start at the beginning. This here is Cayuse. Not very pretty, but don't hold that against him. He'll look after you. So your first lesson will be how to saddle up."

Tilly listened carefully as Ryan went through the order of setting the saddle blanket on the horse's back, then the saddle atop it, and finally which cinch to fasten first and why.

"After riding bareback for so long you might find this uncomfortable at first, but here you go."

He gave her the pony's reins, then held the stirrup for her. Tilly swung up into the unfamiliar saddle. When she settled into it, Ryan adjusted the length of the stirrups for her and made sure she was comfortable before untethering his own horse. He checked the cinches, made a few adjustments, and then quickly mounted. As soon as he'd turned his horse away from the fence, a large, dark brown and very hairy dog came out of the shadows of the horse shelter.

"Is that your not-so-good dog?" Tilly asked with a grin.

"Yup, that's Tuff."

"What is he?"

Ryan laughed at that. "Your guess is as good as mine. A bit of this mixed with a bit of that with some of the other thrown in. He's good around the horses though."

"Where are we going?" Tilly asked as Cayuse followed Ryan's horse.

"I'm taking you over to Vermilion Lakes. It's a nice ride. I think you'll like it."

The traffic in the town seemed to bother neither the horses nor Tuff who trotted along beside them. A few people stopped to watch them ride by, most of them seeming to appreciate Ryan's roan.

"He must be something special," Tilly remarked noting the interest in the horse.

"Yep, he's a Tennessee Walker. I got him down in Montana a couple of years back. Just about the best horse I've ever had, too. His name's Grulla, for his color."

They followed the river for a while and then began to skirt a lake, the horses' hooves making a sucking sound as they pulled their feet out of the soft ground. Tuff darted in and out of the shallows, his paws pattering through the water to the accompaniment of soft splashing sounds.

"This is the first of a series of three lakes." Ryan waved his arm in the general direction of the expanse of water. "There's a hot spring in the third, but we won't have time to go that far today but this is what I wanted you to see."

He reined in and half-turned Grulla to face the lake. Tilly pulled up beside him and looked back. A soft gasp of surprise rushed from her parted lips at the sight before her. Evening sunshine washed across Mount Rundle's ragged peak, tinting it pink. Every line, every splash of color, and every tree on the far side of the lake transferred into a perfect mirror image on its smooth, still surface.

"Look there," Ryan said, pointing to a dark shape at the edge of the opposite shore. "A moose and her calf."

From his shirt pocket he took a pencil and notebook, and began to write in it.

"What are you doing?" Tilly watched him curiously.

"Making a note of the time of day, weather conditions and where she is. It's a habit I learned from Josh, who has to do it every day. Keeping accurate records is part of a park warden's job."

"Is that Josh's job?" Tilly continued to watch him write.

Ryan closed the notebook and put it and the pencil back in his pocket. "Yep. He likes being outdoors even more than I do. He did one shift with Dad in the mine, said never again and joined the Park Warden service. He's out on patrol in the mountains right now and will be for the rest of the summer."

"So what does he actually do?" Tilly shaded her eyes and watched the moose and her calf wade through the shallows.

"Watches for game, checks their health and numbers, makes sure trails are in good order, deals with poachers and timber-cruisers if he has to."

Tilly frowned. "What's a timber-cruiser?"

Ryan chuckled. "Guys employed by the large lumber outfits. They check out and estimate the most likely trees for felling, but it can't be within the park boundaries. Josh sometimes has to re-educate them of where they're at. He's the closest thing to a lawman out there."

The pride in Ryan's voice as he talked about his brother made her smile. Closing her eyes, she inhaled deeply, drawing in the sweet, damp, moisture laden air. All the tension of the day flowed out of her as the utter peace of her surroundings claimed her. When she looked again, the image in the lake had begun to shift as the sun began its slow descent. Pink-tinted clouds formed over the mountains, then fanned out in delicate fingers across the indigo sky.

"So what do you really want to do, Ryan?" She spoke quietly, not wanting to disturb the peace of the evening. "Will being a guide satisfy you, or is there more?"

"Of course there's more." Ryan folded his arms across his saddle horn and leaned towards her as if about to share a confidence. "I want my own place. I want to raise the best trail horses I can because I tell you, Tilly, tourism is not going away. It's going to get bigger and bigger. The Brewster brothers knew that. That's why they invested in automobiles, so they can take tourists on sight-seeing trips, but we're always going to need horses in Banff. Eventually I'd like to run a guest ranch. Think you could handle that?"

Tilly saw the dream in his eyes and began to dream right along with him. "I think so. We could have a house for us, and cabins for the guests."

"And show visitors the best of our country," Ryan continued. "Wouldn't that be grand?"

A soft breeze heralding the on-coming night whispered across Tilly's cheek and made her aware of a subtle shift in the atmosphere. Mist began to rise in the sedges, creeping between the green spears of the reeds, and spreading delicate tendrils across the water's surface. Ripples formed where fish rose to feed on hovering rafts of midges. Further out, in the center of the lake, dark bodies flashed silver as they leapt right out of the water, falling back with a loud splash amidst an arc of spray.

She didn't want to move but the increasing chilliness in the air made her shiver. It was only a slight movement but Ryan asked her if she needed a jacket. She shook her head and picked up the reins, dropping them again as a long, mournful wail drifted across the water. Startled, she looked at Ryan.

"What was that?"

"Only a loon." Ryan cocked his head to one side, intent on the sound. "He's calling for his mate. Listen. He's saying 'where are you?' And now she'll answer."

Tilly heard the call again, but with a slightly different cadence, one call being a slightly higher pitch than the other. The light faded even more and she shivered, knowing they had to leave but not wanting to. Ryan called Tuff who had been nosing around in the low scrub around them and they began the ride home.

They had not taken many paces when, in the distance behind her, the shriek of a train whistle brought a frown to her face. She twisted around in her saddle to peer back down the line. Way down the track, the oncoming locomotive's lights sliced through the gloom like scythes. The hiss and roar of its engine sounded louder and the rails began to whine in protest at its approach.

"That doesn't sound like a regular train," she said.

"Smart of you to notice that." Even in the gloom she could see the smile creep across his face. "It's an express train and will probably have a couple of silk cars on it."

"What are those?"

"The raw silk comes in burlap-wrapped bales by ship from China, usually aboard a Canadian Pacific steamship."

Tilly looked up at him in surprise. "I didn't know they had ships as well as the railway."

"The steamship fleet was another of Van Horne's big ideas." Ryan tapped his temple with his knuckles and grinned at her. "See, you have to be like Van Horne, Tilly, and think big. Their ships have side ports making it easier and faster to load and unload cargo. The silk is offloaded in Vancouver, rushed through customs and loaded into specially designed, airtight boxcars lined with varnished wood, then the bales are covered in paper and the car sealed."

"Is the silk that special?"

"Yes, that's why the cars have to be moisture and thief-proof." A wistful expression crept over his face. "It used to be a huge business, with some trains carrying more than one and half million dollars' worth of silk. They had their own, specialised crews and guards. The trains stopped about every hundred and twenty five miles or so to be greased and lubed and a pit stop averaged just seven minutes."

"Where were they taking it?" The train sounded closer now and Tilly looked over her shoulder, scanning the distance between where they were and the railway line. She hoped the horses wouldn't spook.

"To Toronto, Montreal, and Buffalo. The freight passed through the National Silk Exchange in New York to be traded on to mills up and down the east coast, where they turned it into really expensive fancy goods."

Tilly imagined the feather-like but incredibly strong fabric made up into scarves and lingerie, ties, shirts and dresses.

"That sounds like quite a business."

"It was. At the height of the trade a silk train took precedence over any other train on the line so they didn't have to stop. Even express trains were forced into sidings to let them pass. But the crash of '29 changed all that, like it did everything else, so there's not the same demand for silk now because it's such a luxury item." Ryan halted Grulla and a moment later the train roared past in a cloud of smoke and steam, spewing glowing sparks and cinders into the night.

"So who told you all this?" Tilly asked with a little grin.

Ryan smiled at her teasing. "My brother, Dan. He works for the CPR and was a guard on the last two regular silk train runs back in '33."

As the train flashed by Tilly noticed that three of the boxcars were different.

"Why are those cars shorter?" she asked.

"Those were the silk cars. They were built shorter so they could take curves at high speeds. Dan told me those silk trains were faster than the express trains, and could travel at up to eighty miles an hour. Can you imagine that? These days they are just hitched to regular passenger trains."

Ryan lapsed into silence and Tilly couldn't help but feel he was mourning the loss of an era. She said nothing as she followed him. The horses seemed to know exactly where they were going. Grulla strode out ahead of her, his black legs almost indistinct in the gloom, making it appear as though the rest of his body glided unsupported through the night. She did not have to encourage her pony to keep up—he seemed just as eager to head for home. Tuff kept pace with them, the sound of his panting interspersed with rustling sounds as he dove headlong into the brush following one scent or another.

She was happy to ride in silence, but hearing Ryan talk about his brother Dan she became curious about the eldest brother. Not having any siblings had never really bothered her, but she wondered all the same what it might be like.

The streets were less busy than they were earlier in the evening with many of the stores already closed. Coyotes in the zoo were beginning to sing as they crossed the bridge, and Ryan had to call Tuff to prevent him from darting away. Pools of light from the Mineral Springs Hospital splashed across the road at the junction of Spray and Glen Avenues. They trotted on in the near darkness beside the river.

"We'll go straight to your lodging," Ryan called back to her. "I'll drop you off and then take the horses back."

She could only be thankful that she did not have to walk anywhere on her own and said so.

"You don't think I'd leave my girl to find her own way home, do you?" he asked as they dismounted.

"Am I your girl?" They stood between the two horses, breathing in their warm, dusty, sweaty, scent. Ryan bent his head and kissed her.

"You know you are." His voice held a husky tremor and Tilly thought his hand trembled slightly as he caught hers.

Tilly laid her head on his shoulder and laughed when Grulla turned his long head and nuzzled both of them.

"Go on," Ryan said pushing him away. "No need to be jealous."

She patted the white pony's neck and handed the reins over, but found it hard to leave Ryan. He stood watching her as she approached the door to her building.

"Will I see you tomorrow?" she called.

"Not for a few days," he said. "I've got a couple of over-night pack trips until the weekend. I'll catch up with you as soon as I get back."

He mounted and gave her a final wave as he rode away. She listened for a moment to the fading clip and clack of the horses' hooves and had the giddy feeling that part of her heart went with him.

Happier than she had ever been, she hummed softly to herself as she walked along the corridor to her room. She opened the door and reached in to switch the light on, but before she could, an anguished voice stopped her.

Chapter Fifteen

"Fliss?" Tilly entered the darkened room. It took her a moment to determine the huddled shape cowering in the corner. "What's wrong?"

She hurried to the edge of the bed.

"Is the door locked?" Fliss whispered as another sob shuddered through her.

Tilly assured her it was, but Fliss just sat there with her arms around her knees, rocking backwards and forwards.

"I can't help you if I don't know what's wrong," Tilly said gently. "Come on, Fliss, tell me what happened."

Fliss sniffed. "All right. But don't put the light on. Just open the curtains."

Tilly did as asked, then sat down and waited. Fliss shifted slowly to the edge of her bed and looked up. Ambient light filtering through the window illuminated her pallid face. What made it more stark, more shocking, was the dark pain in Fliss' eyes and the deep purple stain of a bruise on her left cheek. Shocked, Tilly could only stare open-mouthed.

"Who did this?" she asked when she had recovered herself enough to speak.

"Frederic," Fliss stammered and then started to sob again.

"Oh, my Lord," Tilly whispered. "Does Saul know?"

"Not yet." Fliss dropped her head into her hands. "I don't want him to either because I know exactly what he'll do. We can't afford that kind of trouble, Tilly, we really can't."

"I need to turn the light on so I can get a closer look at the damage," Tilly said softly. "I'll close the curtains first and then there's no chance of anyone seeing you."

Tilly reached up and pulled the shabby fabric across the window, making sure there were no gaps before she turned on the light. She put her hand under Fliss' chin and lifted it up.

"Ouch," she whispered. "That's got to hurt, but at least the skin isn't broken. Did he punch you or slap you?"

"Punch." The word slipped from Fliss' lips as a tears trickled down her face.

Tilly nodded. "We had a neighbour who was free with his fists. His wife often had bruises to show for it. There's a deeper bruise just below your eye, probably from one of Frederic's knuckles. I'll get some cold water for a compress."

At home she would have had a bowl or bucket she could have filled. Here the only handy receptacle was a dusty chamber-pot from beneath her bed. She hurried to the bathroom where she washed it out then filled it with cold water. When she returned, Fliss pulled a face at the choice of container.

"Don't be picky, it's the best I can do on short notice," Tilly said as she soaked a face-cloth in the water. "Hold on, this will hurt."

As gently as she could she placed the wadded cloth over the bruise. Fliss moaned and bit her lip but took the cloth and held it place on her cheek.

"Let me know as soon as that needs changing." Tilly dropped another cloth into the pot. She swirled it around, her anger building with each slow motion of her fingers. It was just not right that Frederic could treat her friends like this and get away with. His treatment of Burma was bad enough. If she wanted to she could tell her father. Whether he believed her not would be another matter. But Fliss did not have that luxury. She had no one to turn to.

As much as Tilly believed Saul would defend Fliss the best he could, the simple fact remained that if he showed any retaliation, Frederic could get them both fired. There was no one they could appeal to, no one to whom they could turn for help without creating an even worse situation.

Tilly changed the cloth and sat down again. "I've got some aspirin if the pain's too bad," she offered but Fliss shook her head.

"It's feeling better already." Her voice was still shaky but her sobs had subsided.

"Can you tell me what happened?" Tilly asked.

Fliss swallowed hard. "Saul and I try to be discreet. It's not always easy and I think Frederic saw us together. He followed me and grabbed hold of me. He said if I was dishing it out, he'd have some too. I struggled and managed to kick him, and that's when he hit me. Someone was coming so he let me go and I came straight back here."

Tilly thought for a moment. "Those girls you told me about from last year. Did he hit them?"

"I don't really know," Fliss said, reaching for a fresh compress. "I wasn't friends with them and didn't talk much to either of them—I only know that he caused them problems."

"Then we have to cause him a problem." Tilly's chin jutted forward.

"But what can we do, Tilly?" Fliss reached for another cloth and Tilly wrung it out and handed it to her. "We're just two girls who count for nothing."

"Speak for yourself, Fliss." Tilly sent her a stern look. "I count for something, or at least I think I do and that's all that matters."

"What are you going to do?" Fliss glanced at her warily.

"I'm not sure yet," Tilly said slowly. "I'm going to have to think on it. How's that compress doing?"

They changed it one more time and agreed that Tilly should report to Miss Richards that Fliss was sick.

"She won't believe it," Fliss said. "I'm never sick."

"She will the way I tell it," Tilly insisted. "By the way, have you ever handled mules?"

"What? Mules?" Fliss could not keep the surprise out of her voice. "Why would I? I'm a

133

city girl through and through. I've never been on a farm in my life and, from what you've told me, you'd never been off one."

Tilly laughed. "That's true. But mules are great teachers."

"They're just horses with long ears."

"That is just where you're wrong, missy." Tilly settled herself on her bed, her back propped against the wall. "My dad didn't talk about the war much, but he preferred mules because he said they're smarter than horses. They have more stamina, can manage on less feed if they have to and can carry proportionately more weight than a horse. They can kick forwards, backwards, or sideways. They can be sweet and forgiving or ornery as all get out. It all depends on how you treat them."

Comprehension blossomed in Fliss' eyes. "So if you treat them badly—"

"They will never forget or forgive you." Tilly leaned forward. "You're my friend, Fliss. I won't forget or forgive Frederic Vanderoosten for what he's done to you."

"So, stubborn as a mule really is the truth."

Tilly was relieved to hear Fliss laugh. "But what you have to remember is that a mule is stubborn for a reason. It usually means he's thinking something through. Don't worry, we'll get this straightened out."

The following morning Tilly reported early to Miss Richards's office.

"She's never sick," Miss Richards said, just as Fliss had predicted.

134

"I'm sorry, Miss Richards, but she is." Tilly folded her hands in front of her and tried to look demure. "I'm afraid it might be my fault. We were talking about blueberries and how good they are, but Fliss picked juniper berries, which aren't."

"And you know the difference?" Miss Richards shot Tilly a suspicious glance.

Tilly shrugged. "Yes, but she doesn't. She'd eaten some before I got in and now she has a really upset stomach. I'll take her rooms if you like."

"You will never get through both your quotas." Miss Richards pulled out a staff schedule and ran her finger down the sheet. "You have thirteen regular rooms and Miss Evans's suite. You can take six of Felicity's regular rooms and I'll reallocate the rest for today. And she can make up for today by forfeiting her next day off. Does she have everything she needs?"

"Yes, thank you, Miss Richards, but if I could take some ice for her? She needs fluids to top up—"

"Yes, yes. There's no need for details."

With a wave of her hand Miss Richards dismissed her and Tilly went straight to the kitchen for a bucket of ice. Grabbing it with both hands she rushed back to their room where Fliss waited anxiously.

"Well, what did she say?"

Tilly placed the bucket on the nightstand. "I've got you today off. I'm taking six of your rooms."

"Well for heaven's sake don't make a muck of them," Fliss ordered and then softened her voice and added, "Thank you. What's supposed to be wrong with me anyway?"

"I told Miss Richards you have an upset stomach after eating juniper berries which you thought were blueberries. My fault, of course. I should have warned you." Tilly grinned. "Here, let me have a look at your face."

She turned Fliss' face to the light and thoroughly inspected it. "Hmm. It's better than I expected it would be, but use this ice to carry on with the cold compresses. I'll see you later."

With so much extra work to do Tilly could have done without Burma, who seemed in the mood to talk and followed her around the suite as she cleaned it.

"Why are you in such a rush today?" Burma complained.

"Fliss is sick," Tilly explained. "Apparently she ate something that disagreed with her."

She went into the bathroom to empty the waste bin and noticed several discarded tubes of lipstick and face-cream containers. A thought struck her.

"Burma," she called, "what did you use to disguise your bruises?"

"Tinted pan-cake foundation." Burma came to the bathroom door. "Why?"

"I know someone who has a bruise that could do with some camouflage. You wouldn't be able to spare any of that pan-cake, would you?"

Burma went to her dressing table and came back with a small container. "There you go, courtesy of Mr. Max Factor, Hollywood's top cosmetician. I don't need it back as I brought two of everything. Just apply it with a damp sponge, let it dry and then add more if necessary."

"Burma, you're a star. Thank you." Tilly slipped the container in her pocket and left the room.

By the end of the day she was not only physically exhausted but mentally exhausted. To how many people had she told the berry tale? By now she almost believed the story herself but, all the same, she had to swallow hard when Saul approached her.

"Can I get her anything?" he asked after Tilly had told her story yet again. "Should I go and sit with her?"

Tilly shook her head emphatically. "She's really not up to it, Saul. Between the bucket by her bed and a direct route to the bathroom, she's better off alone."

"All right." Saul still looked doubtful and Tilly hurried off before he could question her further.

She sat with Fliss until late in the evening. When the night shadows crept through the trees, casting long fingers of shade across the paths

137

surrounding the hotel, she dressed in her corduroy pants and laced up her boots.

"Where are you going?" Fliss asked as Tilly pulled on her jacket.

"Just out to get a breath of fresh air, Fliss. Don't worry. I'll be fine."

But she wasn't fine. Her head told her she was being stupid. Butterflies thudded around in her stomach. But she had to find out where Frederic Vanderoosten was, and what he was doing, if she was to figure out a plan to give him a taste of his own medicine. Ryan and Saul had put the word around to watch him, but nothing had come back to her or Fliss of the man's movements, so she doubted their efforts had been productive. Going to Sam's, knowing full well that Ryan would not be there, was a risk she was prepared to take if she could discover anything that she could use.

She stood in the doorway of the bar. Smoke drifted in a blue haze below the low ceiling. Instructions delivered in rapid Chinese and accompanied by utensils being slammed around told her the chef was not in a good mood. She scanned the room, not recognizing any of the packers at the bar and only two of the hotel staff playing cards. Plenty of people had seen her and Ryan together. Any one of them could suppose she was looking for him, including Frederic, who she'd spotted sitting in a back corner.

Her heart hammered as she ducked back outside. Had he seen her? She thought not as he'd been talking with Jeffrey Sachs, both of them laughing and joking with the two ladies from the hotel who she'd last seen flirting with Ryan.

Her thoughts brought a frown to her face as she walked back the way she came. Burma had told her she had broken her engagement to Frederic, but that news had not yet filtered into the gossip telegraph in the hotel. That Frederic was a notorious flirt was common knowledge. Even people who did not much like Burma thought she deserved better. And now, it seemed, Frederic was not even trying to hide his flirtations. Was this something she could use to discredit him? Should she tell Burma what she had seen, or was Burma well aware of her ex-fiancée's behaviour?

Telling Ryan or Saul what had happened would result in nothing but the trouble Fliss so feared. Both men would likely take Frederic out behind the woodshed and give him the hiding he so deserved. She would have to think of something subtle, something that would stick. But what? And whatever plan she devised, how could she achieve it?

Lost in thought, she was not immediately aware of footsteps on the path behind her. But, as the back of her neck began to tingle, she knew who was there.

"Looking for me, were you?" His voice slid over her already sensitized nerves as smoothly as whiskey over ice.

Her pulse thudded in a beat heavy enough to shorten her breath. Her palms became clammy and she shoved her hands into her jacket pockets.

"Not at all." She kept walking. "I was looking for Ryan."

"And lucky you found me instead." Frederic took hold of her arm and tried to push her into the shadow of the trees.

"Leave me alone, Frederic." Her initial fear now turned to cold anger as he continued to manhandle her.

"Why should I?" A nasty tone crept into his voice as she continued to evade him. "You have to know such a pretty thing as you is like honey to a bee. A fatal attraction, if you will, and there's nothing you can do about it."

"No?" Tilly broke free, breathing hard, and took a step back.

Frederic's eyes glittered with excitement. His face bore a feral expression, that of a hunter after its prey as he moved towards her. Tilly took a deep breath. She had stood toe-to-toe with farm boys. Slapping them had been no more than a pat on the cheek, making them laugh and tease her even more. That was until her father explained that men punch and women slap. Then he taught her to punch and the farm boys didn't laugh at her anymore.

Her lungs tightened and her breath shortened as she looked into Frederic's pale eyes.

His laugh held not a hint of humor, more an edge of cruelty as he sneered at her. "Got you a little scared, have I?"

She thought of Burma's necklet of bruises and formed a fist, knowing that Frederic would not be able to see what she was doing in the darkness that surrounded them. She stood her ground and waited.

Frederic took another step towards her. Tilly didn't even have to close her eyes to see the bruise flaring across Fliss' cheek. She tightened her fist.

As soon as Frederic took his next step, she swung her fist up with all her strength. It connected with a solid, smacking sound under the point of his chin. His head snapped back and, with a grunt, he collapsed on the ground.

Panting hard, Tilly shook the pain out of her hand and then leaned over him. His eyes were closed and he was unconscious, but still breathing. A quick look around assured her they were completely alone. There had been no one to see what had happened. As an additional precaution she pulled off Frederic's shoes and set them down an arm's length away from him. Even if he came round quickly, he would not go far without them.

Her heart raced as she hurried home. She had set out to see where Frederic was and what he was doing but achieved so much more. He could not complain about her without revealing his part in the matter. Nor, she suspected, would he want anyone to know he had been knocked out by a girl. But men like him did not give up.

Had she just made the situation better, or worse?

Chapter Sixteen

A few anxious days later, Tilly finally began to relax. Between the cold compresses and Burma's pan-cake make-up, the bruise on Fliss' face was barely noticeable. Saul noticed it, of course, but Fliss brushed it off as having tripped and fallen on the stairs. A perfectly feasible excuse, but one Tilly was not sure he believed. There was no gossip around the hotel, no murmurs of anything untoward having taken place. Wealthy and elegant visitors from Boston and New York, from Chicago and San Francisco, from Europe and the Far East, continued to arrive and depart, all delighted with the size and amenities of the magnificent hotel cradled in the heart of the Rocky Mountains.

All seemed routine, and yet she could not shake off the feeling that something unpleasant hovered on her particular horizon. She had not seen or heard Frederic but sensed he would not leave well alone. She tried to put him in the back of her mind and looked forward, instead, to Ryan coming back from his pack trip.

Would she tell him what had happened? She decided not. He would be angry with himself for not being there to protect her, and then angry with her for taking such a risk.

Hindsight is wonderful, she told herself as she cleaned a bathroom. She was sure that, given the same circumstance over again, she would not have wandered out into the night and dangled herself like a dang carrot. She had been too angry to think straight and, but for being farm strong, might have fared far worse.

Finished for the day, she thankfully stowed her service cart and turned in her uniform. As she started down the stairs she heard music, and slowed her steps, listening carefully. She could determine no particular tune and then realized that the violin, piano and cello strains that drifted up to her were not in tune with each other. Continuing down the stairs, she followed the sounds to the foyer where the trio, which played for the dinner hour, were practicing. She listened for a while longer, quietly humming along when she recognized the sets they played.

She listened to the babble of conversation in languages she did not understand from people walking past her and could only guess at their origins. More and more people came through the foyer and she decided she should go. Taking the stairs, she went down one more flight and exited onto the Garden Terrace. She knew she should not be here but could not help but take a deep breath, enjoying the scent of the blooms on the terrace. For a moment she rested against the parapet and looked down along the valley, sighing at the grand sight of the river below her and the soaring mountains beyond.

It gave her a badly needed lift and now, feeling more settled and at peace with herself, she returned to her room to tidy up for the evening. Fliss was waiting for her and Tilly was relieved to see how much better her face looked.

"All thanks to your administrations and Burma's make-up," Fliss said. "By the way, did you hear what happened to her?"

Tilly shook her head, her curiosity roused by a glint of indignation in her friend's eyes.

"She finished up in the swimming pool, gala ball gown and all."

"Oh, no. Not the strapless, sequinned red gown?"

"That's the one." Fliss settled back against the wall as if ready to gossip. "She was overheard arguing with Frederic. He and Jeffrey and those two hangers-on Sylvia Turville and Cecily Waters were having drinks by the pool before dinner. He said she was drunk, and she said two drinks didn't even make her head swim and if he wanted to see her drunk then she'd show him what drunk was. She called a waiter and ordered a bottle of champagne. She wanted Veuve Clicquot but the waiter told her he could only offer her Dom Perignon or Bollinger. She went off like a rocket about the lack of amenities and what sort of hotel didn't stock Veuve Clicquot and, before anyone knew it, she was in the pool."

"Didn't she know she was so close to the edge?"

"Apparently not." Fliss shrugged. "Although, it's being said she was pushed."

"By the waiter?" Tilly asked.

"Could have been him, could have been Frederic, could have been Sylvia. By all accounts there's no love lost between those two and no wonder at it. No one knows for sure. Frederic offered her a hand up, but she refused and waded to the ladder where she bunched up all her wet skirts and climbed out of her own accord."

"Do you see it happen?"

"No, one of the waiters did and told Saul—"

"Who told you," Tilly finished for her.

Fliss laughed. "Oh, come on, Tilly, that's the kind of gossip that's too juicy not to share. Not only that Saul later overheard Frederic telling Jeffrey that he'd slip a five spot to whoever pushed her if he could find out who it was."

"Poor Burma," Tilly murmured.

"I know she helped me," Fliss said, "but I still can't think of her as anything other than a spoilt rich girl who got what was coming to her. I've seen the likes of her many a time, and they all seem to get what they deserve in the end."

"That's not fair. You don't know what she has to put up with." Despite Burma's haughtiness, Tilly sensed a deep unhappiness in the girl. How could someone have all the benefits that such wealth could provide and still be unhappy? She made an instant decision. "I know it's late but I'm going up to see her."

"She'll probably throw something at you," Fliss warned.

"And will get it thrown right back at her if she does. I'll see you later."

Tilly hurried to Burma's room, knocked smartly on the door and was ordered to go away.

"Burma, it's Tilly. Can I come in?"

She listened carefully as she waited for an answer and heard mutterings and crashes as if Burma stumbled into things. Maybe she was drunk, Tilly thought.

"All right, if you must." Burma slurred her words as she wrenched the door open. Her hair was still damp from her tumble into the pool. Her mascara had smudged, leaving a black trail on her cheeks and appeared to have difficulty in focusing her vision on Tilly.

Tilly stepped inside and looked around in disgust. "Good Lord, Burma, your room is a disaster."

Clothes, as usual, cluttered the floor. Magazines were thrown carelessly beside one chair, and onto the seat of another, as if Burma had begun reading in one place then moved to the other. A couple of bottles of wine and another of champagne in a bucket sat on a side table with an empty glass on floor beside it. The red dress lay in a wet heap in the bathroom doorway.

"Pooh." Burma shrugged and sniffed loudly as she wiped her eyes on the back of her hand, spreading the mascara further astray. "Who cares?"

"Well, I do as I have to pick up after you."

"Poor you."

"Don't be so snide." Tilly picked up the dress, placed it on a hanger and hung it over the bathroom door. "I don't know if we can do anything about this, but I'll take it to Laundry anyway."

She perched on the arm of the sofa and regarded Burma gravely. "Come on, out with it. What happened?"

Burma chewed on a nail and looked as though she would burst into tears. "In a word—Frederic."

"What about him?" Tilly asked carefully. She could not reveal a word of her own involvement with Frederic and hoped that he had not said anything about it either.

"He and that obnoxious Jeffery are hanging out with Sylvia Turville and Cecily Waters. Those stupid girls think they have snagged a pair of gems. I'm not sure which is the worst of the two, Jeffery or Frederic, but it is so humiliating to have one's ex-fiancée dangling a new girlfriend on his arm right under my nose." Burma collapsed on the bed, throwing her forearm across her eyes in a dramatic gesture worthy of a stage performance.

"You know you are better off without him," Tilly said reasonably. "Why are you making such a fuss? I would have thought you would be relieved?"

"I should be, but I'm not." Burma sniffed. "It was such a lovely feeling to be actually wanted by someone. I felt so special when I had his ring on my finger."

147

"But Burma," Tilly said softly, "surely it's better to be wanted by the right person, someone who will love you for who you are rather than what he can get from you?"

"I suppose you're right," Burma said mournfully. "And I still have to explain everything to Papa."

"You still haven't told him?"

"I've tried, I really have." Burma sat up, piled the pillows in the middle of the bed and reclined on them. "But everything is arranged. Papa's secretary has liaised with the catering manager here and organized everything for two hundred guests. The invitations have gone out, rooms have been booked for those who are coming. We've even received wedding gifts."

"So what?" Tilly sat on the end of the bed. "If your father's secretary is so efficient, she can take care of returning those as easily as she sent out your invitations. I'm sure people will understand."

"I'll be a laughing stock," Burma sniffed. "Especially to my bridesmaids who all told me I was acting in too much of a hurry, but I thought Freddy loved me."

"Maybe they knew something you didn't," Tilly said carefully. "Are they here?"

Burma shook her head. "Helen and Ruth are in Italy, Lillian is in France, and my matron of honor, Frances, is in the Bahamas. They'll all be arriving next week and I just don't know what I'm going to tell them."

"The truth, I should think," Tilly offered. "Frederic turned out to be an absolute cad, so you ditched him. It wouldn't hurt to tell them the whole truth either. You might find they have more sympathy for you than you think."

"But how do I deal with Papa? I told you, he really likes Freddy and was so looking forward to taking him into the business. Freddy is the son he never had."

"Have you actually talked to your father?" Tilly asked, suddenly suspicious that Burma might be avoiding him.

"Once." Burma punched a pillow. "He said he had something to tell me but it would have to wait until he got here. He didn't want to discuss it over the phone. Something about wedding rings. I had no idea what he was talking about. Freddy took care of all of that."

"Burma, I could shake you." Exasperated, Tilly stood up. "Are you so used to playing the helpless little woman that you really cannot stand up for yourself? You're pretty and sophisticated, well-educated, and yet you have no back-bone."

"Who made you my mother?" Burma snapped back. Her mouth puckered into a disapproving pout.

Tilly rolled her eyes. "No one. All I'm saying is that you really should try standing up for yourself a little more. Who knows what may come of it?"

"Oh, I suppose you're right," Burma acknowledged ungraciously.

149

"Well, maybe I am or maybe I'm not. What you do is up to you. Right now I'm going to take this dress to Laundry. Can I do anything else for you?"

Burma shook her head and Tilly left the room and headed for the stairs. She preferred them to the elevator. Half way down the flight she heard music again and thought the Toronto Trio must still be playing. She stopped and cocked her head. It sounded more like a full orchestra than the three musicians she'd listened to earlier. Where was it coming from?

It was a waltz, she was sure of it. She followed the sound, stopping when the music faded, following it when the notes became clear again. Picking up the melody, she hummed in time with it and then stopped, surprised to find herself outside the grand doors of the ballroom.

A chilly draft of air swirled around her neck. She shivered as she opened the door and peeked inside, expecting to find an orchestra practicing its repertoire. Moonlight fell through the tall window panes, filtering between the half-drawn, full-length drapes hanging from the swagged valances. The silvery beams made the shadows darker, yet somehow illuminated the gold accented ceiling and the splendid chandeliers.

Puzzled, Tilly looked around. A grand piano with several rows of chairs placed close to it, sat at the conservatory end of the ballroom. Tall potted palms marked each end of the last row of chairs, but of pianist and audience there was no sign. That someone had been there was evident from the pile of sheet music placed on the bench seat at the keyboard.

She could still hear the music. It was louder now, pulsating in her ears, vibrating in her body. She turned around, thinking that maybe someone had turned on a radio or started playing a record on a gramophone. She was quite alone. The music must simply be in her head, but she knew she had never heard that particular piece before.

Shadows suddenly shifted in the center of the floor and the chill drifted over her, making her shiver again. There was nothing she could see that could have caused it, yet the shadows continued to twirl like fall leaves caught in a capricious breeze. A mist formed before her eyes, swirling out of the shadows and spiralling upwards, becoming more and more solid until she detected a wispy, smiling figure who beckoned to her.

That's right, Tilly, come in. Come and waltz with me.

The words echoed in Tilly's brain, resonated through her as clearly as if a living person had spoken to her. A compunction she could not deny drew her into the center of the ballroom.

Details on the bride's dress emerged, shimmering into view—white silk flowers embroidered onto satin. The bride's blonde hair was swept into a topknot with loose ringlets framing her smiling face and tiny tendrils curling at the back of her neck. Her white, elbow length gloves covered slender arms. The music swelled and the bride flowed around the floor, leaning back as if held by invisible arms.

Tilly lifted her own arms. The red dress dripped water onto the floor but she took no notice as she picked up the melody and began to hum along. It was intoxicating. She was laughing now as she and the bride spun around and around, faster and faster as the music roared in her ears. Her feet moved in a blur and did not seem to belong to her. Breathless now, she lifted her arms higher, the red dress lifting and falling like a flag in the wind.

The ballroom doors flew open and a loud voice brought her to a sudden stop. Disoriented, she blinked and stumbled. The music had faded. The bride had gone. In her place stood Miss Richards, red-faced and furious.

"McCormack," she snapped. "What do you think you are doing?"

A flush of embarrassment crawled up Tilly's neck. "I'm sorry, Miss Richards. I don't know what came over me."

"Your behaviour is disgraceful. You have no business being in here." Her sharp gray eyes focused on the dress in Tilly's arms. "Whose dress is that?"

"I was taking it to Laundry for Miss Evans."

"Then you'd better get on with it." Miss Richards walked past Tilly and surveyed the splattered ring of water on the polished hardwood floor. "I hope for your sake that floor is not ruined. Now get along with you."

Almost in tears, Tilly made her way to the laundry. She handed the dress in and had assurances that every effort would be made to restore it, but she barely heard a word.

Her head still spun from her giddy waltzing and she felt a little sick. She needed air. Now.

Chapter Seventeen

Tilly gulped in long, sweet drafts of the cool evening air and waited for her whirling mind to slow down.

Where had that music come from? Why had she been so entranced with it? And why had the bride chosen her to dance with? Had it really happened or was it all her imagination?

Quite apart from the ghostly apparition appearing before her, the music still haunted her. Every note, every chord still swelled within her. She had to find out what it was. Of all the people she knew, only a musician was likely to know, and the only musicians she knew were the gentlemen of the Toronto Trio who played each evening in the dining room. If she ran, she might just catch them as they finished up.

She tore back into the hotel, ignoring the astonished glances of patrons as she rushed by them and raced up the stairs. Her passage would be noted and reported to Miss Richards, she was sure. Panting, she halted at the entrance to the Fairholme Dining Room. Thank goodness. They were still there. They looked slightly formidable, formally dressed as they were in black tail jackets and white bow ties, but Tilly pulled back her shoulders, lifted her chin and approached them anyway.

Mr. Adaskin had his violin case open and was lovingly storing the instrument in it. Mr. Crerar collected sheet music, making a pile easily as thick as the one she had seen on the piano bench in the ballroom. Mr. Ysselsteyn smiled at her as she caught his attention.

"Could you gentlemen please help me?" She licked her lips, now almost too nervous to make her request.

Mr. Adaskin looked up. "What would you like help with?"

His soft, cultured voice encouraged Tilly. "I heard a piece of music which I now cannot get out of my mind, but I don't know what it is."

"How annoying for you." Mr. Adaskin chuckled. "We all get tormented with that from time to time."

"If I hum it, might you recognize it?" Tilly held her breath.

"Why don't we try?" Mr. Crerar had taken his seat at the piano again. "Close your eyes and just let the music take you."

Tilly took a deep breath and allowed her lids to fall. Instantly the music swelled in her ears and she began to hum, softly at first but then as the melody overwhelmed her she began to vocalize the tune. She la-lahed the waltz time, keeping measure with graceful, flowing sweeps of her hands as if she were conducting an orchestra. Gradually she heard the soft, quivering notes of the violin take over, then the tinkle of the piano keys as the gentlemen took up the meter and melody. Mr. Ysselsteyn picked out the lower tones on his cello to complement them and she opened her eyes.

"Oh, that's wonderful," she breathed. "What is it?"

"That," Mr. Adaskin said, smiling as he inclined his head to her, "is the barcarolle from The Tales of Hoffman, the opera by Jacques Offenbach. Where did you hear it?"

"That's just it." Tilly shrugged helplessly. She really could not tell them that she had been dancing to it with a ghost. "I really don't know. It just came to me and is driving me crazy."

"Did you see any of the operas staged in the Cascade Ballroom by Mr. Alfred Heather?" Mr. Crerar asked.

Tilly shook her head. "That must have been before my time. I only started this year."

"Ah, I see. Well, I don't think they ever performed the Tales, but the barcarolle is a Venetian boat song from Act Three of the opera. The rhythm represents the rocking of the boat, you see." He played a few bars of the melody and to her surprise Tilly easily pictured a gondola being poled along a canal. When she looked up he was nodding his head and smiling at her. "There you go, you've got it," he said. "If you can, come and listen to us Saturday night. We're playing in the Mount Stephen Hall and we'll try and slip it into our repertoire in your honor."

"Oh, please don't," Tilly begged. "At least, play it if you like but not for me. I shouldn't have bothered you but do thank you so very much."

"No bother, miss." Mr. Crerar closed the piano lid. "It was something of a challenge but we were pleased to help."

People, having finished their evening meal, began to leave the dining room. One gentleman, a fat after-dinner cigar between his fingers, came up and clapped Mr. Adaskin on the shoulder.

"Well done, Murray. I do believe having soft music playing in the background while dining helps my digestion. Good night."

The couple walked away, the lady's hand tucked into the crease of her husband's elbow.

Tilly thanked the musicians again and wished them a good evening. She took her time going downstairs, admiring the vaulted ceilings above her and the satiny sensation of the highly polished banister rail as it slipped beneath her hand. Art work and artifacts decorated the walls and as she stepped off the last stair she realized she was not far from the Mount Stephen Hall.

She looked over her shoulder. It wouldn't hurt to take a peek at it and to imagine the trio set up in there for their Saturday night concert. There was no other member of the hotel staff in sight, no one to ask what she was doing there or to stop her. She walked into the great hall with its solid wood dining sets and leather upholstered sofas beneath the windows.

Although the hour was late, enough light fell through the panes for her to see the stained glass panels set in them. Her footsteps echoed on the bare flagstones. She marvelled at the span of oak ribs across the ceiling and the ornate chandeliers hanging from the central beam. A small balcony opened out above each arch of the cloister corridor and, wanting to see what the view from them would be, she headed for the stairs.

About to take the first step, she paused. A distinct click, as if one sharp thing had hit another, shattered the silence, followed by the sound of women laughing. Drawn by the sound, she drew back from the stairs and followed the corridor. Light spilled across the hall and, suddenly wary, she kept to the shadows.

"Good break, Jeffrey," one of the women sang out.

"Nonsense, Sylvia," came a voice that sent a shiver down her spine. "He's playing like a duck with a broken wing. Look at that angle. Preposterous."

There was another click and a muffled oath followed by Frederic's insincere, "oh, bad luck."

Tilly knew she was close to the billiard room and ladies' retiring room. She had no wish to be seen, especially by Frederic and started to back away. She had only taken a couple of steps when Sylvia spoke up.

"So tell me, Freddy, are you going to try and make it up with Burma?"

Even at this distance Frederic's exasperated sigh seemed to vibrate through the space. "Her old man will be here at the end of the week so I suppose I'll have to. Shame, though, because I won't be able to play around with you two. I'll have to be a good boy, at least until after the wedding."

"Are you so sure of Burma?" Cecily Waters asked.

"Do you doubt my fatal charm?" As he spoke, an image of Frederic's smug smile flitted across Tilly's mind's eye. "I'll twist her round my little finger just like I did the first time. I'll get togged to the bricks and she won't be able to resist me."

"You'll have to really dress well to impress her," Sylvia said with a laugh. "You are such a cad, Freddy."

"But you love me anyway." Another resounding click and a delighted, "Yesss," from Freddy told her he must have made a good shot.

She didn't wait to hear anymore. Soft-footed, she fled back to the stairs and ran up, thankful that she had not been seen. She stopped on one of the balconies above the cloister corridor and looked down into the great hall below her. Hearing Frederic talking so disrespectfully and callously about Burma made her blood boil.

Now she was in a quandary. Should she tell Burma what she had heard, or just leave well enough alone? She thought she could manage to word a comment in such a way that she could give Burma a fair warning of what to expect. Hearing voices again she stepped away from the wrought iron railing, pressing herself against the solid stone frame. She hoped that none of them would look up as the four of them walked across the floor, the girls' kitten-style heels tapping a sharp tattoo on the flagstones. Sylvia hung on Frederic's arm and Cecily and Jeffrey had their arms about each other. They disappeared from her view and, when she could no longer hear them, she hurried to her room.

For all that she had thought about what she might do, she had come no nearer to a plan to discredit Frederic in Fliss' defence. Maybe she had done enough. Maybe there was nothing she could do. Feeling a little glum, she let herself into her room.

"Where have you been?" Fliss asked, her voice quivering on an anxious note. "I've been worried sick about you."

Tilly slumped on her bed. Her long day had begun to take its toll and she found it difficult to keep her eyes open.

"Sorry I took so long but you will not believe what happened." She scrubbed her hands over her face in an effort to keep herself awake.

"Well don't keep me in suspense," Fliss prompted. "What happened about the dress?"

"The dress?" Tilly frowned, then remembered the whole reason she had gone rushing out earlier that evening. "Oh, yes. The dress. Well, Burma was in a bit of a state, I must admit. She didn't throw anything at me, before you ask. She seems to be really worried about her father's arrival. I guess I was just lucky with my dad. I could talk to him about anything and I was never afraid of him as Burma seems to be of her father. I guess he's too busy making money to give her the attention she needs."

Fliss twisted around and plumped up her pillows. "I certainly prefer love over money but I can't say I wouldn't mind a bit more of it."

"Are we talking about love or money?" Tilly asked as she switched the light off.

"Both," Fliss said with a giggle.

"Oh, Lord, this feels good." Tilly sighed as she lay down on her bed. Should she tell Fliss about the music and dancing with the ghost in the ballroom? She thought she might, but not tonight.

As she hovered on the edge of sleep, Fliss startled her awake.

"Oh, I almost forgot." Her voice echoed in the darkness. "Saul said Miss Richards was looking for you."

Tilly's eyes flew open. She caught her breath as she propped herself up on her elbows.

"And you're only telling me this now?"

"Sorry, but at least I didn't completely forget. What have you been up to?" In a rustle of sheets, Fliss sat up. "Was it something to do with Burma's dress or—Tilly! You didn't mess up my rooms the other day, did you?"

"Not that I know of, no."

Now they were both fully awake again, Tilly knew she would not be able to keep the story to herself. Still not quite believing it and

161

thankful for the shadows to cover her blushes, she described the ghost in the ballroom.

"And there I was, lost in the music and spinning around like a top with my arms full of Burma's wet dress when in walks Miss Richards." Tilly dropped her face in her hands. "I couldn't have been more mortified."

"Did you go and see her after you went to Laundry?"

"She never asked me to," Tilly said. "At least, I don't remember her asking. Saul didn't say what she wanted, did he?"

A loud yawn came from the other side of the room. "No, just that she wanted to see you. It's probably nothing."

Tilly lay down again, but now she couldn't close her eyes. She lay quietly, pleating the hem of her sheet between nervous fingers. Had she damaged the ballroom floor? Had someone seen her talking to the musicians and complained? She mentally reviewed each room she had serviced that day and knew that each had been thoroughly cleaned. Surely there could be no complaints there.

She turned on her side and tried to sleep but, try as she might, she could not settle. Her thoughts soon became a jumbled mess of dresses and brides, of music and Ryan, of mules and mountains. She tossed and turned, was hot then cold. She turned her pillow so that it would be cool beneath her cheek and at last huffed a troubled sigh and gave up and slept.

Chapter Eighteen

Her alarm clock went off long before Tilly was ready to wake up. She hit the 'off' button and peered at the time. The clock peered back at her like a pale, baleful eye.

Still only half awake, she stumbled out of bed and shook Fliss, who was barely stirring. By the time she'd used the bathroom, Fliss had made both beds and opened the curtains. Tilly looked out onto a bright, fresh morning full of sunshine. She hoped it was a good omen of what her day had in store for her.

After they had breakfast, Fliss took off to the sixth floor to start work, and Tilly, heart-in-mouth, presented herself to Miss Richards. The woman was no more welcoming than she had been on Tilly's first day. If anything, she looked more austere and regarded Tilly in glacial silence for what could only have been seconds but felt like eternity.

"McCormack, do you remember what I said to you on your first day here?" she asked when she finally dropped her gaze to some paperwork on her desk.

Tilly raked through her mind for the various instructions she had received that day. There had been so many. "With regard to what, Miss Richards?"

"Don't be so impertinent." Her hard glare pinned Tilly to her chair. "I warned you to not make me regret hiring you."

Her heart thumped uncomfortably and Tilly ran her tongue across her bottom lip. "Has my work not been satisfactory?"

"Miss Taylor appears to have no complaints as to your actual work, but it is your general conduct that is sadly lacking. There is not only the incident I myself witnessed, but several guests have reported you running through the hotel, up and down stairs where you should not be and at times long after your shift has ended. Not only that, your honesty is now under review."

"My honesty?" Tilly stammered. "Whatever do you mean?"

"Miss Turville is missing a valuable diamond ring. You are the only person, other than herself, who has been in her room."

"But I have only been in her room once," Tilly protested. "That was yesterday when Fliss was sick."

"And was she there?"

"Well, no."

"So you had plenty of opportunity to search her belongings," Miss Richards accused.

Anger curled in Tilly's stomach. She clenched her fists in her lap. This, she was sure, had to be Frederic's doing. "Actually, Miss Richards, no, I didn't. My time was fully taken with doing my job and making sure I did all the extra rooms just as carefully as I did my own allocation."

"So you are denying any accusations of theft?"

Her face now flushed with the effort of keeping her temper, Tilly looked directly at Miss Richards. "I most certainly am."

"And you would have no concern if your room was searched?"

"Of course not." Tilly bit off the words before she exploded in a tirade that would not do her any good.

"Very well." Miss Richards lifted her telephone and dialled a number. "Mr. Spence, we are ready now."

Tilly gasped as she looked up. If she had not been sitting she feared her legs might not support her. Mr. Spence was head of hotel security.

"Come with me."

Holding her head high, Tilly followed Miss Richards's long, sweeping stride across the service floor. Mr. Spence met them in the lobby and greeted Miss Richards with a gruff hello. He gave Tilly a long, assessing stare before briefly nodding his head.

The hour was too early for many guests to be about, but there were enough of them. They and the bellhops and receptionists watched the little party pass by with curiosity. Tilly sensed the whispers and knew the gossip train would be building up a full head of steam. She lifted her chin and kept her shoulders back. She had done nothing wrong, had nothing to be ashamed of.

She opened the door to her room and stepped aside to let Miss Richards and Mr. Spence enter.

"My bed is the one on the right," she said, "and I have the bottom two drawers in the dresser."

Mr. Spence first pulled apart her bed, expertly searching the bedding and mattress. Tilly bit her tongue. If she had been so stupid as to steal a ring in the first place, she would not compound her stupidity by hiding it in her bed, but it would not do her any good to say so.

She watched as her belongings were pulled out of the drawers, shaken out and thrown on her bed. Fear and anger changed into indignation, but she kept quiet.

"Have you anything else?" Miss Richards asked.

"I have a jacket and a coat in the armoire and two boxes under my bed." Tilly folded her arms tightly across her stomach. It was becoming increasingly difficult to keep her temper. She could not accuse Frederic Vanderoosten of any wrongdoing without disclosing her own involvement with him. And what repercussions would there be if she allowed that to happen? She knew how cruel and manipulative he could be. Had he coerced Sylvia Turville to help him? That was just the sort of thing she could imagine him doing.

Having finished searching the armoire Mr. Spence knelt and pulled the boxes out from under her bed. There were a few magazines given to her by departing guests and a couple of books in one, her spare monthly toiletries and some make-up in the other. Miss Richards looked at her with hard, narrowed eyes.

"I take it this is your own make-up?"

"Yes, Miss Richards," Tilly said in a tone tight from clenching her jaws together. "That is for occasional use when I go out."

"And what about this?" Mr. Spence held up a small, round tin. It looked like a decorated pill container but the closest thing to a pill she ever took was an infrequent aspirin for monthly stomach cramps.

"That's not mine," she said firmly. "I've never seen it before."

Mr. Spence shook it. It rattled ominously. Tilly held her breath while he removed the lid. He looked inside the tin then held it out for Miss Richards's inspection.

"McCormack, how could you—?" Miss Richards tipped the tin into her palm and held up a ring. Even in the early morning light, the rose gold band glistened softly while the diamonds, clustered into a turban design, caught every vestige of light and winked mockingly at her.

Tilly shook her head slowly.

"No," she said, weathering the accusing stares from two pairs of eyes. "I have never seen that ring before."

167

"Then how do you account for it being found amongst your belongings?" Mr. Spence got up and brushed the dust from the knees of his pants.

"I have no explanation for that." Tilly vibrated with anger. "I am not here for more than half the day. Anyone could have come in and hidden it."

"And yet the ring went missing the day you were in Miss Turville's room, and is found in your possession today," Mr. Spence continued. "Something of a coincidence, wouldn't you say?"

"Too much of a coincidence," Tilly blurted out. "I have no doubt that someone is trying to make it appear that I am a thief. I can assure you I am not. And even if I were, would I really be so stupid as to hide something that valuable in my own room and then agree to your searching it?"

Mr. Spence rubbed a hand along his jaw but said nothing. He glanced at Miss Richards, a glance in which his doubt was all but spelled out. Tilly narrowed her eyes. There was something more going on here, something she was unaware of and not privy to. Another thought came to her. She had never seen Burma wearing her engagement ring. What if Sylvia Turville's ring was not the only one to go missing? What if there was more? Wouldn't that indicate that there might be thief at the hotel?

"Well?" When no comment was forthcoming Tilly looked from Mr. Spence to

Miss Richards. "May I tidy my room and go to work?"

Miss Richards looked nonplussed, and Mr. Spence simply shook his head, as if to say any decision made would have to be hers.

"I think it best, McCormack, that you resign your post here," she said quietly. "There appear to be some anomalies that need to be considered, but I have to satisfy Miss Turville that I have taken appropriate action. As the ring has been recovered, she may not press charges. I know you have no home to return to and because of that, I will permit you to stay here until you can find another position. Accommodation only. You will not be permitted to enter the hotel again. Do you understand?"

Tilly nodded wordlessly and closed the door behind them. Tears of frustration stung her eyes as she looked at the wreckage of her meager possessions strewn across the beds. Mr. Spence had not been the least bit tidy in his search. Was that something of a punishment for his having to do it? Her mind whirled as she began to pick up and fold her clothes.

Without a word being said, without any direct contact, Frederic had discredited her more quickly and thoroughly than any plan she could have devised for him. She had crossed him in the most humiliating way, and this was his revenge. She had no doubts at all about that. She sat on the edge of her bed and covered her face with her hands.

She had no family or home to go to. After all he had done for her she did not want to have to contact Mr. Bentinck for help. Miss Richards wanted her to resign, which meant the hotel management would not pay her fare to anywhere. She doubted there would be a reference to help her get another job.

Miserable though she was, something else bothered her. How had Frederic known who slept in which bed? She knew Fliss would never have told him anything. That meant someone had spied on them, or had already been in their room to find out that information. Staff came and went at all times of day and night depending on their shifts. There was always someone about but the thought was not a comfortable one.

She'd finished sorting through her belongings, and packed most of them, when Fliss came rushing in.

"I can't stay long, but I've just heard the news," she said. "Tilly, this is awful. I know you would never have done such a thing. Is there anything I can do?"

Tilly shook her head. "Not unless you know where I can get a job and a home all rolled into one. Miss Richards said I could stay here for now, accommodation only. I could starve before I find something else."

"Why don't you try The Dominion Cafe or the Paris Tearoom?" Fliss suggested. "They're both on Banff Avenue and busy enough that they might take you on as a waitress."

"Not without a reference, they won't." Tilly sighed. "I wish Ryan was back."

"Look, I've got to go." Fliss gave her a quick hug. "Don't do anything rash. I'll see you later."

Once she was alone again Tilly quickly changed into her pants and boots. If she was going to have to find another job, she wanted one out doors. She emptied the small change from her purse, counting the coins into her palm. Just enough for a meal and coffee.

The morning had gone from being bright and clear, to cold and misty. She pulled up her collar against the chill and pushed her hands into her pockets. Before she went anywhere, she would go to the Brewster's barn.

Right now the only person Tilly wanted to see was Ryan.

Chapter Nineteen

The smell of horses and hay, leather and rope in the dimly lit barn reminded her of home. She stood just inside the doorway, listening to the stomp of hooves as horses shifted in their stalls and their soft snorts of curiosity as they sensed her presence. She took a few more steps, drawing comfort from the old familiar smells that enveloped her.

Headstalls and bridles, cinches, ropes, and chains covered one wall. Beside them hung an assortment of chaps and slickers with an untidy pile of boots beneath them. She guessed anyone could take what they needed, when they needed it.

"Can I help you, miss?"

Tilly turned around, not sure where the man had sprung from or how he had managed to approach unheard. He was a little more than her height, and surveyed her from a pair of eyes almost as blue as her own. He'd crammed his hat firmly on his head and pulled up the collar of his denim jacket to his ears, as she had. Dusty denim pants covered a pair of bandy, skinny legs that declared him to be a life-long horseman.

"I'm hoping you would know when Ryan Blake is due back."

"So you're his girl are you? Heard you were a pretty one. Put it there." He stuck out a none-too-clean hand and Tilly shook it, noting the calluses and broken nails, the nicks and small scars. "Like some coffee?"

"I'd love some," Tilly said, warming to the man.

"Come with me then." He scurried along the aisle between the stalls and Tilly followed him. "We don't exactly have an office, but here's where most of the paperwork gets done and the coffee made."

Tilly followed him into a space holding a desk, a couple of chairs and a stove. The coffee pot sat on top the stove, and she warmed her hands while her new-found friend took two mugs off a shelf and poured the coffee.

"No fancy fixin's here, miss," he warned as he handed her a steaming mug.

"Strong and black is just fine." Tilly smiled at him and sat down. "Thank you, Mr....?"

"Nugent. George Nugent, but just George will do." He raised his mug to her before taking a sip, and she wondered how he could drink it so hot without even blowing on it.

"Would you be Billy Nugent's father?"

"I am that." George lifted his mug again. "Knowed you met him, 'cause it was him told me about you. Seems like you got young Ryan hog-tied from the get-go and I can see why. And you can't wait for him to get back."

Tilly looked up into those blue eyes and felt comforted by the warmth she saw there. "Yes, I'm in a bit of bother and need to talk to him."

"Bother?" The blue eyes narrowed. "He's not treated you disrespectful, has he?"

"Oh, no, nothing like that." Tilly blushed as she understood his meaning. "It's just that I'm not going to be working at the hotel anymore, and I'm hoping he might know where I might get another job and somewhere to stay."

George rubbed his hand over his chin. His day-old bristles made a rustling sound under each rub. "Kin you handle a pitchfork 'n brush a horse?"

"Yes to the pitchfork," Tilly said with a smile, "but I'm more used to mules than horses."

"Are you now?" George cocked his head, looking at her with interest, then smacked his mug down on the desk as if making a decision. "Come with me."

Tilly took another quick sip of her coffee before following George to one of the stalls.

"This here's Molly," he said as he stood aside for Tilly to look in.

Standing with its head down in the corner was the most dejected looking animal Tilly had ever seen.

"She's lost an awful lot of condition." Tilly ran a practised eye over the jutting shoulder blade and just-showing ribs. "What's wrong with her?"

"She's mournin'."

"Oh, dear." Tilly edged into the stall, aware of the fact that a mule could kick not just backwards, but forwards, and to the side as well, but the mule never moved. "Who is she mourning?"

"Her cat. She's been pals with a three-legged stray we've had around here for years. Darn thing goes off every now and then and comes back with a belly full of kittens. She always has them in Molly's stall, but this time something went wrong. She died a few days ago after birthing just one. I found it in the morning and Molly's been off her feed since. Only lips at her water and hasn't even tried to bite me."

"That bad, huh?" Tilly moved up to the mule's shoulder. "You poor girl. I know what it's like to lose someone you love." She laid her hand on the mule's neck and saw the slightest twitch in one of Molly's ears. "It's too bad we can't explain things to you."

She continued to talk quietly, ran her hand over the dark brown hide then scratched along the top of the mule's neck. There was no response from Molly.

"If you want a job," George continued quietly, "help me get her interested in life again. She's a good girl and I'd hate to lose her too. We've got a couple other barn cats round here for mousing, but Molly don't take to any of them, and they're all toms anyway. Maybe 'cause you're female she might just connect. Will you give it a try?"

Tilly nodded as she continued to run her hands over Molly's shoulder and back. "Have you got a brush I can use?"

"Sure." George shuffled off and came back a moment later with a bucket of grooming tools. "Can't do anything 'bout a place for you to stay right now, but the boys might know of something round town."

"Thanks, George." Tilly produced a shaky smile as she selected a brush from the bucket. "I'll stay with her for a bit, and then I'll start on the stalls. Do you want them done in any particular order?"

"Nope, though it'll be easier to do the empty stalls first. Pitchforks and barrows are in the hay stall opposite the office."

He tipped his hat and she heard his boots scuffing on the floor as he left her and the mule alone. Tilly continued with the stroking and scratching then started working the brush down the mule's dark brown neck.

"Missing your kitty, are you?" she said softly. One of the long, hairy ears swivelled slightly. She swiped the brush down Molly's neck again. "I know what that's like. I loved my dad and my mom and miss them like crazy. I try not to let it show because it's nobody's grief but mine. Dad's not been gone long, but I was only seven when mom died. She'd lost two babies already when she got caught with a third."

Tilly ran the brush down Molly's shoulder, following with a long sweep of her hand. The mule's hair was soft and a little dusty. She continued brushing and blew softly between her lips so that she didn't get any of the dust in her mouth. Brush. Hand. Shush. She repeated each movement slowly and steadily, noticing that Molly had dropped a hip and nearly closed her eyes. Her long, dark lashes fluttered as she blinked sleepily.

"Dad treated Mom like a queen," Tilly continued, "and we did everything we could so that she could just rest, but then the baby came early and she started bleeding. I'll never know if I had a brother or a sister, because mom died with the baby still in her. By the time the doctor came out from town we'd buried them. So you see, I understand how sad you are."

Tilly buried her hands in the mule's thick, stiff mane. Tears for all she had lost coursed down her cheeks, ran off her chin and dripped onto Molly's neck. She quickly scrubbed her face dry with the back of her hand.

"See, we're not so different, Molly," she whispered into the mule's ear. "So I'll just cry for the both of us."

Startled by a noise in the aisle, Tilly look over her shoulder. Was George there? Had he heard her? She hoped not. She gave Molly a final pat and fetched a pitchfork and a barrow. The job George had given her was a routine that came to her easily but, before long, she was warmed enough to remove and hang up her jacket. The work continued down one side of the barn and then she started back up the other. She even found it easier than she expected to

177

work around the horses, finding that the big Percherons and the pair of Belgians were especially amenable. She had just finished cleaning a bay gelding's stall when George called to her from the aisle.

"You'd better come see this, miss, 'cause I'm not quite sure I'm seeing it myself."

She peered around the gelding's hindquarters, only to see Molly, with her ears pricked, looking out of her stall. Tilly went to her, put her arms around the animal's neck and gave her a hug.

"Don't know what you said to her, but I reckon she's payin' you attention. Could be just a girl thing though." George grinned at her. "I pity those poor boys if they have to contend with you two."

"Go on, George, you're just teasing." Tilly grinned back, enjoying the moment. "Those poor boys, as you call them, are quite able to stand up for themselves."

George had made another pot of coffee and Tilly was happy to take a seat in the snug little office. She looked up at the clock on the wall, surprised to see how quickly the day had passed.

"Ryan's due back any time now." George's little smirk told her he'd guessed why she'd been checking the clock. He poured more coffee. "Tell you what, when he gets back, I'll take care of his party and he can come talk to you."

"Thanks," Tilly shook her head. "But if I know Ryan he'll want to do all that himself."

A clatter of hooves made them both look out of the office. The big blue roan horse almost filled the doorway and Tuff came running in, his tail wagging as he greeted her and George. Tilly heard Ryan laugh and then, amidst several other voices, Billy joined in.

"Sounds like another bunch of happy customers," George said as he ruffled the dog's ears. "They're dentists from Seattle who are all keen mountain climbers. Wasn't sure how it would work, seeing as this was Ryan's first trip as a guide."

Tilly looked at George in surprise. "I didn't think he was going to do get his guide's license until next year."

George shrugged a shoulder. "We had two guides out already, but I didn't want to let the customers down and figured those two could handle it." He winked at her and grinned. "We'll take care of the paperwork later."

She followed George outside where the party milled around, shaking hands with Ryan and Billy and generally seeming well satisfied. A bearded, bespectacled, gentleman left the group and strode towards George.

"Just wanted you to know," he said, "what a fine young man Ryan Blake is. Bit of a walking encyclopedia, but I learnt more about the area on this trip than any other. Make sure you keep him on, because we want him again next year."

"I appreciate that, sir." George touched a finger to the brim of his hat, acknowledging the compliment. "And just so's you know, I have no intention of letting him go anywhere."

The gentleman nodded and returned to his group while George beckoned for Tilly to join him.

"We'll leave the packs to the boys," he said, "but you can help me take care of these horses. Think you can do that?"

Tilly nodded and stepped up to help unsaddle the horses before turning them into the corral. A cold wind had blown up and they shuffled around before settling themselves alongside the corral fence, using it as a windbreak. George looked up at the sky.

"I'd say they got back just in time. Looks like a storm's blowin' in."

Clouds had dropped over the mountain tops, obliterating the peaks and boiling down into the valleys. Tilly shivered as she walked into the barn where Billy and Ryan were checking the contents of a pack. Both looked up at the sound of her footsteps.

Ryan took one look at her and pushed the pack-horse out of his way. "What's wrong?"

The worry in his eyes almost started her crying again. "Everything and nothing."

"She needs to talk to you, lad," George said. "Go use the office and I'll finish up here with Billy."

"Thanks, George." Ryan put his arm around her and Tilly leaned in to him. Just the warmth of his body made her feel everything would be all right. She looked in on Molly as they passed her stall and was relieved to see the mule munching on a stack of hay.

"You and your darn mules," Ryan teased as he hugged her.

She sat down by the stove while Ryan poured coffee. She shook her head when he offered her the mug and he sat it on the desk.

"I've been drinking coffee since I got here this morning. It was pretty strong then, and I don't think I could handle it now."

Ryan pulled out a chair and sat facing her while Tuff lay down under the desk. "Tell me what happened."

"Do you remember telling me that Frederic Vanderoosten was as mean as a rattlesnake?" As soon as she mentioned the name, Ryan stiffened and Tilly caught his hand and gave it a squeeze. "I'm all right, really, but I did something that made him mad and he struck back in a really sneaky way. He got me fired by having me accused of stealing a guest's ring. Now I've got no job and nowhere to live. I don't know what to do."

"We'll sort something out," he assured her. "First, somewhere to stay. It's not much, but you can use our bunk house. Pete's still out with a week-long pack trip for another couple of nights, and Billy and I can bunk down in the barn here. But what did you do?"

"I can't tell you all of it, not yet, but I found out that he'd hurt Burma. They'd had an argument and he almost throttled her. Her neck was badly bruised. Fliss had warned me that he had a bit of a reputation from last year and to stay out of his way. I thought I had, but he followed me and threatened me and...," Tilly paused and swallowed hard. "I punched him and knocked him out."

Ryan's mouth fell open as he looked at her in wide-eyed surprise. Then he started to laugh.

"It wasn't funny—," Tilly snapped, but his rolling laughter gradually relieved her tension and she managed a small smile. "Well, maybe it was a little bit funny. It was certainly the last thing he expected."

Ryan stood up and pulled her up with him. "So now I know what I'm up against."

"Do you still want to marry me now you know I have a temper and a fist to match it?"

He kissed the tip of her nose and whispered, "More than ever."

She put her arms around him and knew she was right where she belonged. She could have stayed right where she was, but the telephone rang.

"Darn it," Ryan muttered and reached for the disobliging instrument. He listened for a moment and then handed her the telephone. "It's Miss Richards."

Tilly took the handset as if it were going to bite her and hesitantly put it to her ear.

"Hello?"

Miss Richards didn't waste any time returning the greeting. "Tilly, we have a little problem. It may have something to do with this morning, or it may not." There was a slight hesitation then the words came in a rush. "Miss Evans is missing and Felicity thinks you might know where she has gone."

"Why would Fliss think I'd know that?" Tilly asked.

"Apparently you spent a great deal of time with Miss Evans." Disapproval fairly dripped down the telephone line. "Do you have any idea what her plans were? Did she mention cancelling her wedding? Her father is arriving tomorrow and I don't know whether I should telephone ahead and warn him, or simply wait until he gets here."

At the mention of Mr. Evans, Tilly had a sudden thought. "Burma wanted to go to a place called Sundance Canyon, but I don't know where it is. Could you wait one moment?" Ryan had caught her eye and gave her a thumbs-up sign. Tilly spoke into the telephone again. "One of the guides here knows where it is. We'll go out there and see if we can find any sign of her."

Promising to keep in touch, Tilly ended the call and followed Ryan out of the office. "Is it far? Can we drive there?"

"No, it's not far. Maybe a couple of miles, and no, we can't drive there. It's a trail." Ryan strode to the door of the barn and looked outside. He slapped the door frame in frustration. "We'll have to ride and take a pack-horse too."

"Why would we have to do that if it's only a couple of miles?" Tilly came to stand beside him.

"For one thing, it's late in the day." He hooked his thumbs into the belt loops on his denims as he faced her. "For another, the temperature's dropping and I won't risk being caught in the open without gear. Another couple of degrees colder and it'll be snowing."

The instant the words were out of his mouth, the first white flakes began to fall.

Chapter Twenty

"But it's only August!" Tilly stepped outside and held out her hand. Each flake, as light as a feather and as big around as a fifty-cent piece, alighted on her palm and immediately melted.

"You're in the mountains now." Ryan tugged his bandana up under his chin and buttoned his coat. "The weather can change in the blink of an eye. You'd better button up too, and put your gloves on. I don't want you with hands so cold you can't feel or hold on to anything. Grab hats and slickers for yourself and Burma while I get the horses ready."

The thud of a hoof as it connected with the wooden partition, then the clang of a bucket rolling in the aisle, drew Tilly's attention. Molly's furry ears were pricked as she watched the activity with bright, dark eyes. She began to bray loudly, her flanks sawing in and out with the effort.

"Looks like she wants to go with you," George commented. "Too bad I don't have a saddle that will fit her."

"That doesn't matter," Tilly said. "I'm used to riding with just a saddle pad tied on with rope. Can Cayuse carry a pack?"

"Sure he can, but I'd rather have him saddled." Ryan reached beneath Grulla's belly and caught the cinch. "If we find Burma, I'm sure she'd appreciate the ride. I can take what we need in the saddlebags and tied on to the saddles."

Between them, George and Billy transferred items from the pack-boxes into the saddlebags then tied bedrolls and tarps onto the saddles. Tilly bridled Molly and threw the saddle pad and a blanket onto the mule's back, securing it with a girth George took from a driving harness. Ryan tied Cayuse's lead rope to his saddle horn then mounted Grulla.

"You all take care. I'm sure you'll find Miss Evans in fine fettle," George said as he waved them all off.

Tilly wasn't so sure about that as they set out. She had everything she needed. A sturdy mule, warm clothes, and a considerate guide. What did Burma have? Hopefully, she at least dressed appropriately and maybe had a rain slicker and some food in a backpack.

They passed the Cave and Basin, the gray stone walls surrounding it almost obliterated now by the fast-falling snow. Ryan had his head down but, unlike her it, was not to protect her face, but to look for any tracks, any sign that Burma had come this way.

"She might have followed the trail that's below this one," Ryan said, "but we should be able to pick it up where the two join."

He rode ahead, scanning the ground on either side of the trail. Tuff, his thick coat beginning to collect snow like a blanket, trotted along behind Grulla. Where the trails met, Ryan halted and dismounted.

"What's the matter?" Tilly watched anxiously as he peered at the ground around him.

"I can't see any trace of her and this snow's not helping because it's settling too fast."

Tilly reined Molly to one side to let Ryan pass as he backtracked. He muttered to himself as he scanned the trail for any sign of Burma. Tilly said nothing. Surely Burma wouldn't have gone off trail, would she?

"I don't know how I could have missed this." Ryan sounded disgusted with himself. "See here in the mud on the edge of the trail? It's a bit sheltered by this overhanging brush and hasn't collected much snow. These footprints are small enough to be hers. She's gone into the bush, darn her. Whatever could she have been thinking? Doesn't she know it's not safe out here for a lone hiker?"

"Likely not." Tilly waited while Ryan, having picked up Burma's trail again, swung up into Grulla's saddle. "The trouble with Burma is that she doesn't think."

"And that's going to get us in a whole lot of trouble." Ryan continued squinting at the ground. "Ah, here's the same footprint coming back out of the bush. I think this is her trail." Tilly looked where he pointed and saw the narrow print, the heel deeper than the toe. "Does that look like it could be a print from any of her shoes?"

Tilly tried to picture all the boots and shoes she had seen in Burma's closet. "She has a pair of brown leather lace-up boots with a little heel. I think she used those for walking."

Ryan nodded. "That sounds likely. There's not much daylight left, but I can see her tracks now so we're heading in the right direction. Are you doing okay back there?"

"We're fine. Thanks for looking after us."

Ryan looked over his shoulder. He wore his loopy little grin, the one that did silly things to her heart.

"If it was just you, I'd say you're welcome, but that Burma Evans is a pain in the rear end."

"Don't be mad at her." As annoyed as she was with the New York City girl, Tilly didn't want Ryan to think badly of her. "She has a lot more to put up with than you may imagine. It's not entirely her fault and right now I understand why she wanted to be alone. She has a lot to work out."

"Sure." Ryan sounded totally unconvinced. "How to spend Daddy's money, for one thing."

Before Tilly could begin to explain what she knew of Burma's relationship with her father, Ryan held up his hand. Tilly halted Molly while Ryan peered at the ground.

Then he looked up and gave Tilly a full grin, the flash of his even, white teeth heartwarming in the gray afternoon. "I don't think she can be too far ahead. Don't worry. We'll find her."

They plodded on, the horses' hooves almost silent in the snow blanketing the ground. Tilly would have appreciated the sight of it settling on the trees, etching the firs like lace and delicately fringing the river's edge if their mission had not been so urgent.

Neither of them spoke as they traveled beside it for awhile. The slow slide of the current caught Tilly's eye from time to time, but then the trail curved away from the river, cutting deeper between the trees, which seemed to press in on her and deaden all sound.

By now, snow had settled on Ryan's hat and shoulders, and dusted Grulla's rump. Cayuse trudged along beside the big horse, occasionally breaking into a shuffling trot to keep up with him. She had no sense of time passing, nor did she notice the breaks where smaller trails cut off to the left or the right of the trail they were on.

The silence seemed absolute. Looking ahead and around her, Tilly thought the dark shapes of trees seen through the snowfall looked like sentinels. Snowflakes pattered gently across her cheeks and hung on her eyelashes. She lost track of time but then a new sound tugged on her awareness, the rush and splash of water somewhere to her left. There was urgency to it, as if it had somewhere to go and was in a hurry to get there.

Ahead, Tuff stood in the middle of the trail, barking and wagging his tail. She pushed Molly to catch up with Grulla, who had lengthened his stride and was surging ahead.

"We're close to the canyon," Ryan called back over his shoulder. "It sounds like Tuff's picked up on something."

The temperature had dropped a few more degrees and Tilly shivered and pulled her collar up to her ears. The trail was easy enough to follow but she wished Molly could stride out as effortlessly as Grulla had done. Tuff barked again and, as she turned a bend in the trail, she saw him and Ryan beside a still, crumpled form.

They were on the far side of a creek, which fell in cascades between high canyon walls. Rocks and fallen timber littered its course. Tree trunks formed barriers through which the water trickled then gathered volume before plunging to the pool below. Molly splashed through one of the pools and dug her narrow hooves into the bank to scramble up the other side. Tilly flung herself off the mule's back and ran to crouch beside Ryan who was tying his bandana around Burma's head.

"Is she alive?" Her voice cracked with worry as she looked at Burma's white face.

"Yes, but unconscious," Ryan said. "She has a gash on her temple and bruises on the side of her head. Her nose has been bleeding and she's probably got a concussion. I reckon she slipped in the creek because she's soaking wet and cold."

"What do we have to do?"

"Get her out of these clothes and get her warm first." Ryan looked around, squinting at the surrounding rocks and the stands of trees. "We'll make camp over here." He pointed to a level patch of ground between the trees.

"Aren't we going to take her back to the hotel?" Tilly asked.

"I'm not moving her anywhere until she's warm," Ryan insisted. "Tilly, come and sit with her. Take your gloves off and hold her hands but don't rub them. Tuff, come here. Lay down, boy. Now, spread your slicker over her and Tuff. I'll bring another tarp."

Tilly did as he asked, fanning the skirt of her slicker over Burma and the dog. Ryan came back with a the tarp, which he spread over them.

"This should help keep some heat in there." He tucked the tarp around her. "It won't be much, but better than nothing and it'll keep you dry."

He went back to Grulla and took his rope off the saddle. This he slung between three of the trees, looping it around the trunks, and then hauling on it to pull it tight.

"What's that for?" Tilly asked.

"I'm fixing the rope so I can throw a tarp over the one line to make a shelter, and tether the horses to the other. We're close enough to home that they're just as likely to head that way, whether I hobble them or not."

A small, soft moan fluttering between Burma's lips caught Tilly's attention. She laid her hand on the girl's cheek, but Burma showed no signs of regaining consciousness.

"Is she all right?" Ryan called as he fetched more rope and a handful of spikes from one of the saddlebags.

"All I can tell is that least she's still breathing." Tilly looked up as Ryan unfolded a tarp, hung it over the rope with a short lip at the front and a long, sloping back. He worked fast, tying the front down and then fixing the floor. When he'd finished securing it he came across to her.

"How are you doing?" he asked.

"My hands are freezing and Burma is shivering. I can't believe how cold she is," Tilly said through chattering teeth.

"Hang in there, I'm going to collect wood and will soon have a fire going."

"What—?" Tilly almost forgot how cold she was. "Ryan, please don't leave us alone. I couldn't bear it if Burma died and I was on my own with her."

Tears filled her eyes. The last person whose hands she had held like this had been her father. The memory flooded back. She remembered with piercing clarity the sound of his last, rasping breath, the soft slip of his features as they fell into deathly repose, the moment when his body completely stilled.

"Tilly, we're going to be here all night and we need heat quickly." Ryan laid a comforting hand on her shoulder. "You're under cover for now and Tuff won't leave you. I'll be back as soon as I can."

With her heart hammering in her chest, Tilly watched him lead Grulla off between the trees. Cayuse and Molly objected to being left behind and shuffled around restlessly, lifting their heads and tugging at their tethers. Tilly hoped neither of them broke free. Snow continued to whisper softly to the ground around her. It pitched on the back side of the shelter, then slowly slipped off with a moist sigh.

After what seemed an age she heard the crash of breaking twigs, the clip of a hoof hitting a rock, and the chink of harness. Grulla appeared and, from the way he leaned into his breastplate and dug his hooves into the ground, she knew he towed something heavy. He snorted and tossed his head when he came to a halt, and she could see the logs hitched to his saddle. Ryan untied the logs, and tethered him alongside Cayuse and Molly and then came across to her.

"I'm just going to get some firewood now. I won't be long, so don't worry," he said and then set off between the trees again.

How could she not worry? Every time he left her line of sight, she wanted to shout her fear and frustration. Out here, alone, with Burma unconscious and shivering violently, what could she possibly do but worry?

She breathed a small sigh of relief when he returned with an armful of firewood, which he dropped close to the logs. She thought he must have enough, but he reached into one of the saddlebags and produced a hatchet. He inspected a nearby sapling, and then another. He cut both of them down, trimmed them, and pounded them at a slight angle into the ground.

"What's that for?" she called.

"It's for a backplate." He stacked some of the logs up against it. "Once I have the fire going, this will deflect the heat towards the shelter, and help dry the wood out, too."

"How are you going to light wet wood?"

"I've got twigs and Spanish moss from underneath the boughs where it's dry."

He set two of the longer logs across three shorter ones, then packed the top seam with the twigs and moss. He pulled his notebook from his shirt pocket and tore out several pages, which he added to the kindling. When that was done, he angled the third log into place atop the other two. He struck a match and, as it burst into flame, he held it to the paper at several spots along one side of the fire. As the paper caught, he moved around and started on the other side. Thin plumes of smoke spiralled upwards, quickly followed by little licks of flame, which brightened the surrounding gloom.

"Just a couple more things, then I'll be ready to move you all." He gave Tilly an encouraging smile as he passed her on his way to the creek, where he kicked a couple of rocks loose. He considered them carefully before picking them up and carrying them to the fire.

He placed them along the side facing the shelter. "This will stop the logs from rolling as they burn down. I think two more will do it."

He picked up another two rocks of about the same size, placed them and then came back to her. "How's Burma doing?"

"Breathing more steadily I think, but I'm worried," Tilly said. "She hasn't come round yet and she's still shivering."

Ryan nodded. "That's good. It means she's still alive. I'm just going down the trail to cut some fir boughs. I'll be right back."

Moments later the thunk of a blade biting into solid wood echoed back to her as Ryan hacked off one bough after another. Attacking trees had been the last thing on her mind when they had set out on their search, and Tilly cursed Burma every which way for putting them in the position they were now in.

Grulla snorted when Ryan returned the camp dragging the boughs behind him. then set them tip to cut end until they formed a thick bed on the floor of the shelter.

"Nearly done," he said as he laid them tip to cut end on the floor of the shelter, making a thick bed. He came to her and took the tarp off her, gave it a good shake and laid it wet side down on the fir boughs. "A blanket and a bedroll on top of these will make you and Burma toasty in no time."

"What do you mean, me and Burma?" Tilly asked warily. "She's the one who needs the heat."

"Yes, and in her state the best way out here is skin-to-skin."

"Nu-uh, not mine." Tilly shook her head. "No. I can't. I mean, I've never—"

"There's no time for modesty," Ryan snapped. "Burma needs warmth, and quickly. I'll carry her over and you can help me strip her."

Shocked at his abruptness, Tilly bit back a sharp retort as he lifted Burma and carried her to the shelter. He laid her down on the open bedroll, unbuttoned her coat and peeled it off. Her right arm flopped like a dead weight. Taking off her sodden sweater, the reason for it was immediate and shocking.

Her shoulder was swollen and misshapen.

"Damnation. That's all we need," Ryan muttered. "She must have dislocated it when she fell."

"I know what to do, I think." Tilly knelt down and felt Burma's shoulder, letting her fingers read the damage beneath the cold skin. "Sometimes calves can dislocate a hip when they're being born. My dad taught me how fix 'em."

"But Burma's not a calf," Ryan's face screwed into an anxious expression.

"No, but a shoulder is a ball and socket joint, like a calf's hip joint. Same principle." Tilly caught Burma's wrist in both her hands and angled her arm away from her body. "Ryan, I need you to hold her very tight. I have to pull this arm down until it slips back into place in the

196

socket but it takes traction. Do not on any account let her move."

With a grunt of effort, Tilly began to pull the arm. Perspiration beaded on her upper lip as she continued the pressure. She continued to pull and then a dull sucking sound indicated the arm had slipped back into position. She wiped the back of her hand across her mouth and blew out a sigh of relief.

"Now I have to strap it. Have you got another bandana?" She shrugged out of her slicker and jacket as she spoke and took off her shirt. Ryan went to his saddle bag and brought her another bandana. "Between these two I can bind her arm to her body. She'll have to lay on her left side but I think it will be all right. Thank goodness she was unconscious."

"God, I hope we haven't taken too much time." Worry creased Ryan's forehead as he looked closely at Burma's deathly white face. He removed the last of her clothes, and Tilly closed her eyes against Burma's nakedness. Other than her own, she had never seen so much bare skin before and she blushed. It seemed not to bother Ryan at all.

He settled Burma on her left side facing the fire and pulled the bedroll around her. ""Now you," he said. "Strip down to your skivvies and I'll tuck you in with her."

"Why couldn't it be your skin?" Tilly shivered as she removed her pants and slid into the bedroll. The shock of Burma's icy skin against her own made her shiver. How could she possibly warm another body when she herself felt so cold?

"Because," Ryan explained as he pulled the bedroll over both of them and threw a saddle blanket over the top, "I need to collect more firewood. We're going to be here all night, Tilly. Now snuggle up close to her, and spoon her."

"Spoon her? What are you talking about?" Tilly couldn't stop her teeth from chattering as she held Burma's shivering body close.

"Haven't you ever spooned anyone?" Ryan asked.

"No, I've never slept with anyone, so why would I?"

"Oh, that's right. You don't have siblings." He lifted the blankets enough to pull Burma's knees into a right angle. "Put your knees in behind hers, right close."

When he'd readjusted the blankets, he whistled softly and Tuff came up, wagging his tail and licking Ryan's face. "Yep, I know. You're a good dog. Get in there, boy. Lie down."

Despite the snow on his coat, Tilly immediately felt warm from simply having the dog's bulk behind her.

"You'll be all right for a bit," Ryan said, "but Burma's body will suck the heat out of yours and you will shiver as much as she does. Don't worry. It'll be uncomfortable, but it's normal."

"What's normal about today?" Tilly asked. She heard his soft chuckle and blinked back her tears as the sound of his muted footfalls faded away.

Behind her she could feel Tuff's steady breathing. A lead shank rattled as one of the horses shook its head and their hooves shuffled restlessly in the snow. She lifted her head and noticed that Ryan had thrown slickers over their backs. They must be cold too. As she cuddled Burma's body closer, she became colder and colder. Her jaws ached from clenching them to stop her teeth clicking together, but she could not control the quaking in her limbs, which became more and more violent as Burma continued to shiver.

"Burma, please don't die," she whispered. "You can be a real pain, but you're my friend and I need you."

She lay still, listening to the quiet hiss of the snow falling between the trees, and the constant splash and babble of the water flowing down the creek. Burma moaned and Tilly snuggled closer to her. She had never been this close to another person. She supposed her mom had cuddled her, but she really couldn't remember. Her dad had given her an occasional quick, awkward hug. She knew he loved her, and had never looked for more from him, but had gained most of her comfort from being close to the animals on the farm.

But being this close to another, living being? A smile curved her lips as a thought struck her. What would it be like to have Ryan spoon her? Would she like it? The smile grew wider. Yes, she would. She closed her eyes, but moments later they flew open when she heard the crack of a twig and heavy footfalls.

"Are you okay in there?" Ryan asked as he stacked another armful of logs.

She heard the concern in his voice. "Never better," she lied. Her teeth still chattered and tremors ran down her and Burma's bodies, gaining in severity until they both shook uncontrollably.

Ryan ran his hand over her hair. "It won't be long before you'll begin to feel warmer."

Tilly couldn't imagine ever being warm again. Ryan lifted the edge of the blanket and heat from the fire blasted over them. Between that, and the dog at her back, the shivering slowly passed and she began to feel drowsy. Ryan stacked another log on the fire and she wrinkled her nose at the smoke's pungent, woodsy smell.

"I've never seen a camp fire set like that before," she said.

"It's a long fire," Ryan explained. "The heat radiates outwards rather than up. I learnt how to build it from one of the Norwegian skiers the Paris boys had staying with them a couple of years ago."

Tilly stifled a chuckle. "Of course you did. Are those boys anything to do with George and Ida at the tearoom?"

She felt his grin and then heard his soft laugh. "You've got it. Herb and Ted are twins and then there's Cyril, and they have the right idea."

"What's that?" The logs had caught well and were burning steadily. Heat wafted into the shelter, settling over them like another blanket. Burma had stopped shivering and now Tilly began to relax.

"Well, in the winter I run a trap line and cut ice. Those boys guide parties of skiers. I don't see the attraction myself, but if people will pay for it, why not?" Ryan busied himself around the fire, feeding it and keeping the flames steady. "We could keep the guest ranch open year round by offering the same service, even run dog sled teams, too."

"This guest ranch idea of yours gets bigger and bigger." Tilly smiled at his enthusiasm.

"I told you, you have to dream big." Ryan leaned into the shelter. "I'm going to put a hot stone by your feet, so don't kick out. How's Burma feeling?"

"Warmer, I think. Her breathing seems to be steadier, too."

"Good, that's real good." Ryan reached in and laid his hand on Tilly's cheek. "You did good today. I'm proud of you. Now see if you can get some rest."

Rest, thought Tilly. I've got a half-dead girl in my arms, it's snowing like it's the middle of winter, and he wants me to rest.

But the day had taken its toll and before long she drifted into sleep.

Chapter Twenty One

When Tilly awoke, she lay for a time with her eyes still closed. If anyone had ever told her she would sleep so well on a bed of fir boughs and blankets, she would not have believed them.

But something had changed. Burma's breathing was slow and steady, that of deep sleep rather than her previous unconscious state. The shape at her back was different, too. Larger, longer, and more solid than Tuff. An arm had been thrown around her waist and the sound of light snoring vibrated in her ear. She wanted to giggle.

When had Ryan crept into the shelter and laid down with them? She didn't care. She simply cared that he was there. Despite the circumstances, she suddenly felt at peace.

"Is there a reason I'm lying naked in your arms?" Burma asked in a cracked, husky voice.

Tilly's eyes shot open. She sent up a silent prayer as her heart bumped a thankful beat.

"I'm saving your life," she said as calmly as she could. "The least you could do is say 'thank you'."

"Yes, but where are my clothes?"

Ryan stirred behind Tilly and mumbled, "Glad to hear you two girls seem to be back to normal."

"I wouldn't call this normal." Burma wriggled and stretched her legs, and then cried out in pain. "Ow, ouch. Oh, my God, what happened to me? And what's this?"

With her free hand she felt the make-do bandaging that secured her arm against her body.

"You were wet and freezing and had a dislocated shoulder when we found you," Tilly explained. "Ryan said skin-to-skin is the quickest way to warm a cold body."

"So why couldn't I have his skin next to mine?" Burma whined.

"Because he had to do things I couldn't," Tilly said sharply. The thought of Burma and Ryan lying naked together sent a surge of jealousy shooting through her. "Like strip your clothes off and then build that fire."

"If my clothes are wet, what am I going to wear? And what's this?" Burma put her hand up to the bandana on her head.

"You're not out of the woods yet, Burma, so keep still," Tilly advised. "You've had a bad crack on the head and might have a concussion. Can you remember what happened?"

"Right from the beginning, or when I fell?"

"Just from when you fell will do." Tilly had no wish at that moment to hear anything other than the facts.

"I wanted to climb up to the top of the falls. It didn't seem very far, and I thought it might be easier if I went over the rocks, rather than up the trail. How wrong could I be? They were more slippery than I thought and I got wet, so turned to make my way back and then fell."

"You were lucky you didn't drown," Ryan said brutally. "What on earth possessed you to hike out here in this weather anyway?"

"It was lovely when I set out." Burma's voice sounded strained. "How was I supposed to know that it would snow?"

Ryan clambered out of the shelter and stretched before tending the fire. He set another log then turned to the girls. "I've sent for reinforcements. Tilly, you get dressed first and then help Burma. I'll only lend a hand if you need me to."

How could he have sent for help? Tilly frowned, but then realized that Tuff had gone. Ryan must have sent the dog back to the barn. She shimmied out of the bedroll, thankful for the heat from the fire radiating over her bare skin. Ryan tactfully turned his back and busied himself with a pot set on stones embedded in the embers at one end of the fire. The aroma of fresh, boiling coffee stirred her senses. She dressed quickly, laced up her boots and crawled out from beneath the shelter.

Yesterday's storm had already passed, leaving the sky as sharp and clear a blue as if someone had beaten it clean on river rocks and hung it out to dry. Already, thawing snow dripped off the trees, pattering softly around her. She stretched and thankfully took the coffee Ryan handed her.

"If you two could stop making eyes at each other, perhaps you could help me." Burma struggled to sit up and groaned. "Oh, my head. I'm so dizzy and I feel sick."

Ryan came to her and supported her back. "That's because you're concussed. Just sit still, Burma, and try and catch your breath."

Burma closed her eyes and turned her face into Ryan's chest. As the pain passed she relaxed in his arms, and then asked about her clothes.

"They aren't quite dried out yet," he told her. "I've got a dry shirt, pants, and socks right here and you should get into them before the boys arrive."

"Oh, yes. I'll just spring to my feet, shall I?"

"There's the girl I know and love." Tilly smiled, set her mug down and knelt down beside Burma. "Sarcastic as ever."

She helped Burma get into Ryan's shirt, aware that her bound arm would be painful, then helped her stand so that she could step into the pants. Burma swayed as Tilly pulled them up.

"This is so embarrassing," Burma whispered.

"Better be alive and embarrassed than being carted out of here dead." Tilly finished buttoning the waistband but, as soon as she let go, the pants slipped down to Burma's knees. She looked up at Burma's shocked expression and giggled. "You look ridiculous. Hang on, I'll pull them up again and you'll have to hang on to them." She turned to Ryan. "Have you got a belt?"

"Not a spare, but hang on and I'll cut a piece of rope."

Tilly continued to giggle as she threaded the rope Ryan handed her through the belt loops on the pants and tied it in a firm knot. "There. Your dignity shouldn't suffer too badly now."

"So how are we getting out of here?" Burma asked as Tilly helped her into a dry jacket.

"You'll have to ride out from here, but I asked for Billy to bring the wagon as far as he can, so that won't be too far away."

Burma sniffed as she looked at the animals still tethered to the line.

"I am not riding that mule," she announced.

Tilly laughed. "Not good enough for you? Don't worry, Burma, Molly is my ride. You'll be riding the pony."

"That's nearly as bad." Burma continued to grumble as she wiggled her toes into the socks Tilly held for her. "What about—"

"No." Ryan stopped her before she could say anymore. "Grulla is my horse and you are not riding him."

Tuff's barking caught their attention and, a moment later, the dog splashed through the creek and ran up to Ryan. He ruffled Tuff's ears and Tilly cocked her head to one side at the squelching, slopping sound of hooves plowing through the melting snow. She breathed a sigh of relief when Billy and Pete appeared through the trees.

"Nice camp." Billy looked around as he drew rein and dismounted. "Too bad we didn't join the party."

"Some party." Ryan grinned and shook Billy's hand. "Thanks for coming out. Good to see you too, Pete. Where'd you come from anyway? I thought you were out for another couple of days."

Pete nodded. "The weather started to turn, so our guide gave the party the option of staying out or turning back. They wanted to come back. Guess I got in just in the nick of time."

"That you did." Ryan glanced at Burma. Even though she was now on her feet, she was still pale and unsteady. He lowered his voice. "We need to get this gal to the hospital as soon as possible. She's still suffering from a pretty bad concussion, she dislocated her shoulder, and I'm sure her body temperature is still too low."

"Damn, that's a heap to deal with," Pete said. "What do you want us to do?"

"Stay here and strike camp. Where did you leave the wagon?"

Pete hiked his thumb over his shoulder. "There's a flat spot just a couple of hundred yards downstream. We brought horses 'cause we didn't know for sure just how far out you all were."

Ryan frowned as he planned his next move. "I'll take the girls to the wagon and get Burma to the hospital. You sent a message to them that we're bringing her in?"

"Sure did, boss," Billy said, "and brought the extra blankets you asked for. That darn dog of yours sure made a ruckus when he turned up at the barn and, I must say, he writes a note almost better'n you do."

"Yeah, right." Ryan laughed. "Okay, we'll get Burma aboard Cayuse. Pete, ride to the wagon with us and then you can bring Cayuse back here to help carry the gear."

Tilly kept Burma out of the way until Cayuse was saddled and ready, but the pain in her shoulder caused her to catch her lip between her teeth. Billy and Ryan waited until the spasm had passed then helped her mount Cayuse. The pony's ears twitched, but he stayed quite still as she settled herself into the saddle.

"Now you, Tilly." Ryan boosted her onto Molly's back. "Come up close on Burma's left side so you can support her if you have to, and I'll lead her."

When he mounted Grulla and moved up on Burma's right side, Tilly saw just how tall the horse was. It was a sorry party that splashed through the creek. Grulla, anxious to go home, tossed his head and Ryan steadied him.

"Please don't tell my friends I rode an old pony," Burma croaked.

Tilly grinned, thankful to hear Burma's voice. "You can tell them yourself and, if you're not nice to Cayuse, you can darn well walk."

"You are so mean." A moan drifted from Burma's lips and she whispered, "It hurts, Tilly."

"I know." Tilly could only imagine the pain Burma must be suffering and reached across the gap between them to steady her. "It won't be for much longer, and you'll be more comfortable in the wagon, I promise."

When they reached it, Pete and Ryan helped Burma out of the saddle and into the wagon bed. Between them, they settled her in the bedroll and pile of blankets Pete had made ready for her. Ryan had brought some of the hot rocks from the fire in a leather satchel, and now laid these along side of her legs. Tilly scrambled in beside her, grateful for the extra warmth from the stones and the blankets she carried. Pete tethered Molly to the back of the wagon, then swung up onto his own horse, picked up the pony's reins, and headed back to the camp.

Once he was satisfied that Burma was as comfortable as they could make her, Ryan tethered Grulla to the wagon and climbed up onto the driver's seat. He picked up the reins and the pair of Belgians hitched to the wagon started forward. As soon as it moved, a tremor of pain pulsed over Burma's face.

"Hold on, Burma." Tilly reached under the blankets and gripped her hand. Burma simply nodded and closed her eyes, her nostrils pinched as every bump and jolt sent pain through her, her mouth a straight, tight line to prevent any sound from escaping.

"Cry if you want to," Tilly whispered. "I won't tell."

"I almost don't care," Burma muttered. "My head feels worse than it did yesterday, but all of me hurts so much."

"We'll be at the hospital soon and they'll probably give you something for the pain." Tilly gave Burma's had a squeeze. "You're doing great, and just think what a story you'll have for all your New York friends. 'Socialite Burma Evans rescued from the wilds of Banff' will be the talk of the town."

"There should have been a bear." Burma tried to laugh. "Much more dramatic, don't you think?"

Although she had said it wouldn't be long, it seemed like an eternity before the wagon reached the Cave and Basin. From there, the trail joined pavement and the wagon rolled along more smoothly. The news of Burma's accident must have already spread, judging from the number of people gathered at spots along the road. Ryan clicked the team to a steady trot and drove them straight to the Mineral Springs Hospital on Spray Avenue. As he pulled up beside the steps leading to the entrance, a hospital orderly came out and hurried to meet them.

"Hello, Mr. Convie." Ryan jumped down from the driver's seat. "You got my message?"

"I certainly did, Ryan." The man looked over the side of the wagon. "What have we got here then? The lady got herself into some trouble, did she?"

While he and Tilly moved Burma to the tailgate of the wagon, Ryan quickly described how they'd found her and what they had done. Ryan lifted her down, but she stumbled and cried out.

"Put your good arm around my neck," Ryan ordered. Burma didn't argue as he lifted her and carefully carried her up the steps.

Mr. Convie ran ahead and opened the door for them. Tilly would have followed Ryan into an examination room, but a Sister stopped her.

"Are you family?"

"No, I'm her friend," Tilly said firmly.

"Only family is permitted to be with her at this time."

"But she has no family here," Tilly insisted.

"I'm sorry, those are the rules." The Sister closed the door with a decisive click, leaving Tilly, fuming, staring at it.

When Ryan emerged he gave her a hug. "You've done all you can for now. We'll come by later and see if we can visit her then."

She nodded and let him take her to the wagon, where she climbed up beside him.

When they arrived back at the barn, Tilly was dismayed to find a reporter from the *Crag and Canyon* newspaper waiting for them. Ryan waved him away and hurried Tilly into the barn, but not before a camera flashed, capturing the moment. Tilly's knees buckled and, before she knew it, Ryan had scooped her into his arms and carried her into the office.

He sat in the chair by the stove and cradled her in his lap. All her strength had melted away leaving her as limp as a wet rag.

"I hope I never have to do anything like that again," she whispered. "Do you think Burma will be all right?"

"She's in the best place to get well again," Ryan said. "But what about you? What do you need right now?"

"Oh, a hot bath and a soft bed would be lovely, but I'm not that lucky."

"I think that could be arranged." Ryan kissed the top of her head. "George's wife will look after you."

"What?" Tilly looked up at him. "George has a wife? I thought he lived here."

Ryan laughed at that. "That's what it seems like, because he lives so close. Come on, Mrs. Nugent is waiting to make a fuss of you. Seems she always wanted a girl, but just got Billy. Think you're okay to walk a couple of blocks?"

She set her feet on the floor and stood up. The warmth and comfort of the last few moments were enough to revive her a little. Ryan took her hand and walked her to a small house on Otter Street. Petunias bloomed in a pot on the step, a bright spot against the dark timber walls. White curtains hung at the windows and, in answer to his knock, the door swung open invitingly.

"Oh, look at you, you poor lamb." Tilly found herself drawn into a motherly embrace, the kind she had only ever dreamed of. She turned to Ryan, but Mrs. Nugent was already waving him away. "You come and have a cup of tea, my dear. Much better for you than that wicked coffee George brews. I swear he does it to annoy."

Tilly sat in a cozy chair beside the stove, inhaling the aroma of fresh baking and warming herself even more with the tea poured for her. She admired the pretty chinaware, drawing a beaming smile from the older woman.

"George said you'd likely want a hot bath when you got back, so I've got one ready in the other room. Just needs topping off."

"But I haven't got any clean clothes," Tilly said. "All my stuff is still at the hotel."

"Don't you worry about a thing." Mrs. Nugent smiled at her. "George figured it all out for you. He went up to the hotel and spoke to that Miss Richards and your friend, Felicity. All your things are in the spare bedroom."

Whatever she had expected, this was not it. However temporary this arrangement might be she would make the most of the situation. When Mrs. Nugent left her, Tilly quickly undressed and stepped into the steaming tub. Bathing in the middle of the day was an unheard of luxury. She didn't rush, but savored the gently lapping water as she lathered herself with lavender-scented soap. She rested her head against the back of the tub and closed her eyes. How deliciously decadent.

When the water began to cool, she sat up and hauled herself out, reaching for one of the fluffy towels beside the tub. Everything had been placed in the exact spot to make it easy for her. She towelled herself dry and smiled at the sight of her clean clothes piled on the chair.

Once dressed, she returned to the kitchen where Mrs. Nugent had set a plate piled with still-warm cookies and scones.

"Ryan will be back to see you soon. Better help yourself before he can get his greedy paws on them."

Tilly bit into the best ginger cookie she had ever tasted and said so.

"It's the blackstrap molasses," Mrs. Nugent told her as she sat down at the table. She suddenly looked a little serious. "I don't want to pry, my dear, but it seems from what George told me that you're in some kind of trouble."

Tilly licked a cookie crumb off her lip and looked up. George and his wife hardly knew her. Heck, they didn't know her at all and yet they were offering the kind of help she'd only ever dreamed of. She couldn't lie to them.

"I was suspected of stealing a guest's ring which was found in my room." The accusation still stung. "Because of that I was put in the position of being fired or resigning, so I resigned. But I didn't do it, I promise you I didn't."

"Of course you didn't." Mrs. Nugent reached across the table and patted her hand. "Now, if you'd like, we have a spare bedroom since Billy moved in with Ryan and Pete. He said I fussed too much, but I'm his mother, so I think I'm allowed. If you'd like that room, it's yours."

"But I don't have a job," Tilly protested. "I wouldn't be able to pay you any rent until I find something."

Mrs. Nugent threw up her hands as if to fend off Tilly's objection. "Your room and board is paid for two weeks. That should give you time to get settled into some sort of job."

"How? Who paid that?"

"You worked all day at the barn yesterday, didn't you?"

The smile on Mrs. Nugent's face told Tilly all she needed to know and she smiled back. This, she thought, might have been a moment she could have shared with her own mother. She had been so long with only her father for company she had forgotten how comforting a motherly presence could be. They sat at the table chatting quietly, Tilly sneaking more cookies and making Mrs. Nugent laugh. By the time Ryan came for her, she felt quite at home.

He arrived in a buggy and drove her out to the hospital. Tilly was too full of grateful wonder to want to talk, and Ryan seemed perfectly at ease with that. He said he'd wait for her, and Tilly climbed up the hospital steps without a backward glance, knowing he would.

She approached the reception desk and asked if she might see Miss Burma Evans, half expecting to be refused again. To her surprise, she received a beaming smile and directions to Burma's room. She tapped on the door and was asked to step inside. When she did, the powerful scent of roses almost overcame her. There were seemingly dozens of pink, red, and white blooms. Some were in vases, others in bowls set on the windowsill, and on the top of a dresser set against one wall.

Burma sat propped up in bed, with piles of white pillows behind her. She had a sticking plaster on her head, her arm in a sling and a big, bright smile on her face.

"Well, you look much better than I expected you'd be," Tilly said as she took a chair beside the bed.

"It's probably the morphine they gave me." Burma shrugged and grinned at her. "I honestly don't feel a thing."

"So they'll keep you in for a few days?"

"Yes, Papa has insisted." Burma sank back against her pillows. "You know, Tilly, I so underestimated my father. He knew all along that Freddy was a thief, which was the reason he wanted to deal with all the wedding arrangements himself. That was so he could keep an eye on Freddy and be quite, quite sure of his facts before telling me giving me the choice of going ahead with the wedding, or cancelling it. That was why he wouldn't talk to me on the phone. For about the first time ever, we had a proper conversation, and I fully admit to having no idea exactly what Papa has always tried to do for me."

"But what made your father suspect him?" Tilly still

"Freddy showed Papa a diamond pin that he said he'd bought for me. But Papa recognized it immediately, as he'd actually had a hand in designing it. You see, Freddy and I had been to a house party back at Easter. The house where it was held was that of Papa's closest friend and business partner, and the pin had been a gift for his wife. When Papa asked them to check, the pin was not where it should have been."

"But what happened to Frederic?" Tilly wanted to know. "If your father knew him to be a thief, why didn't he just have him arrested?"

"Papa said there wasn't enough proof as there were over a hundred guests at that party. Any one of them could have taken it, or given or sold it to Freddy." Burma shrugged, as if the incident was now of no merit.

"Do you know where he is now?" Tilly asked.

Burma shook her head. "He was apparently seen boarding a bus to Calgary. Papa says there is a warrant out for his arrest, so it's only a matter of time before he's picked up. I'm told your Mounties always get their man."

Tilly laughed. "Yes, that's true, but I'm so glad you were able to talk to your father. You must have had a lot to catch up on."

"Yes, we did. Not that it's any of your business." The glint in Burma's eyes belied her brusque response and she wore an air of smug satisfaction, as if she had a secret but was not quite ready to reveal it.

The uncomfortable feeling that she'd missed something occurred to Tilly but, before she could ask any questions, the door opened.

The tall, well dressed, and imposing figure who entered the room almost took her breath away. Without thinking, she stood up, mouth slightly agape. From everything Burma had said, Tilly had imagined a narrow, mean-faced man, not this clear-eyed gray-haired, handsome individual. His clothes were of the best quality, and his jacket had been cut exactly to fit his broad shoulders.

"Miss McCormack, it's a pleasure to meet you." He held out his hand and Tilly took it. It was warm, and firm, and engulfed hers. When she finally plucked up enough courage to look at him, she detected a wicked twinkle in his eyes. "Not quite what you expected?"

"No, Mr. Evans, you're not," she said, lifting her chin. She glanced at Burma who seemed to be enjoying the moment immensely.

"I told you she was honest, Papa," she said with a laugh.

"And that's a good thing." Mr. Evans smiled at Tilly. "Please sit down, Miss McCormack, it was not my intention to interrupt your visit." Tilly sat down again, still a little shocked by this man, who now walked around to the far side of the bed and took his daughter's hand.

"I'm very glad you are here, though, as I want to thank you profusely for saving my daughter's life. Is there, perhaps, something I might do for you in return?"

"Why, absolutely nothing at all." Tilly looked at him in astonishment. Rescuing Burma and having her survive was thanks enough.

"I told you she'd say that, Papa," Burma said smugly.

"So do you want to tell her?" Mr. Evans looked at his daughter expectantly.

"No, but I will ask her."

Tilly curled her fingers together nervously. "What are you talking about?"

A grin split Burma's face and she looked well pleased with herself. "I talked to Papa about it this afternoon, and I'd like to give you my wedding. Everything has been ordered and paid for. Why not just leave it as it is, instead of having Papa's secretary cancel everything?"

Mr. Evans regarded Tilly solemnly. "I think it's great idea, Miss McCormack. Burma tells me you have no family and, if you should like it, I would be honored to give you away."

The blood drained from Tilly's face, right down to her feet leaving her cold. Burma, looking very pleased with herself, hummed the strains of the wedding march. Then, and much to her chagrin, blood returned to Tilly's face again, burning her cheeks.

"I couldn't," she gasped.

"Yes, you could," Burma said. "You know you're going to marry Ryan and everything's arranged. Wedding dress. Bridesmaids. Minister. Reception." She held up a finger as she listed each item. "Invite who you like."

Too stunned to talk, Tilly just sat there as Mr. Evans headed towards the door. "That's something I'll leave you two to talk about. Right now, I'm going down to have a word with your young man, Miss McCormack."

He left the room and Tilly could do nothing but stare after him.

"Please close your mouth and say something," Burma chided her.

"I don't know what to say." Tilly flapped her hands helplessly, overwhelmed by their generosity.

"Just say yes," Burma urged her. "It will please Papa and me. You saved me from a fate far worse than either of us could have imagined. We know Frederic framed you when he stole Sylvia's ring and had it put in your room. I bet you could even get your job back here if you wanted it. But you don't, do you?"

Tilly couldn't find the words to express what she was feeling. There seemed to be none suitable for the occasion and she gulped awkwardly. "The dress," she finally stammered. "You're so much slimmer than I am. It wouldn't fit me, and your wedding day is only a week away."

"I was bigger when I had that dress made," Burma assured her. "It was only all that nonsense with Freddy that made me lose weight. There are seamstresses at the hotel who can fix it. You'll be fine. Just say yes, Tilly. Please. It would make me so happy."

"I would," Tilly said, "but I can't."

"Why ever not?" Burma slapped her good hand down on the bed in exasperation.

"Because," Tilly wailed, raising tear-filled eyes, "Ryan hasn't asked me to marry him."

Chapter Twenty Two

Tilly ran down the hospital steps, trying to compose herself.

It was all too much. First she lost her job in the worst circumstances. Then she spent the night in a make-shift shelter, hoping to save her friend's life. Her return to town had been marked with the possibility of a new job and definitely a new home. And now her friend's dream wedding had been presented to her as a gift of thanks, all to no avail because of the take-charge all-action man waiting for her by the buggy.

She loved Ryan. She knew it. But she would not be taken for granted.

'I'm going to have to marry you', he'd said and confirmed that statement with, 'I still want to marry you'.

Even Fliss and Burma took it for granted that she would marry him.

She climbed into the buggy with barely a glance at him and ignored his welcoming grin.

"Uh-oh," he kidded as he climbed in beside her. "Am I in trouble?"

"No."

"That means yes." Ryan took up the reins and slapped the horse into motion. "Tell me what I've done to make you look like you've got a mouth full of sour suckers."

"Nothing."

"Liar."

Tilly sat and fumed. No matter what she said, Ryan would have an answer or a comeback for her. "If you must know," she finally said, "Burma and Mr. Evans offered me her wedding. But I couldn't accept."

"Why not?" Ryan almost pulled the horse up in his surprise. "Mr. Evans seemed to think it was a great solution rather than cancelling everything, and what better start could we have?"

"Everyone seems to have thought of everything," Tilly snorted, "except for me. I couldn't accept the gift, Ryan, because, as much as everyone expects it and has taken it for granted that we'd get married, I couldn't because you haven't asked me."

Ryan did pull up then, right in the middle of the Banff Bridge. He got out of the buggy, went around to Tilly and held out his hand. She hesitated for a moment before she took it and stepped down. He took her other hand and held them both in a firm, warm clasp. Right there, beneath a moon that hung like a wish in the night sky, he went down on one knee.

"Matilda Margaret McCormack," he said softly. "You have to know how much I love you. Will you do me the honor of becoming my wife?"

"Oh, Ryan, you silly man," she whispered as tears of happiness slipped down her cheeks.

"Why couldn't you have done that in the first place? Of course I'll marry you."

He pulled her into his arms and set about kissing her, not with the gentleness of their first, shy kisses, but with demanding delight. She threw her arms around his neck and kissed him back, would have kissed him again but the rumble of the buggy moving caused them to break apart.

The horse, too close to home and tired of waiting, had taken off. Ryan raced after it and hopped aboard, halting the horse while Tilly, laughing, caught up and clambered onto the seat beside him. She tucked her hand beneath his arm, and dropped her head on his shoulder. Utter happiness made her feel dreamy and as light as air.

"Will you tell Burma and her father yes tomorrow?" he asked when he dropped her off at the Nugent's house. "I could never give you such a grand wedding, Tilly, and you deserve it."

Smiling up at him, she nodded, kissed him goodnight and then let herself in to the kitchen where Mrs. Nugent sat knitting. She looked up over her half-spectacles and dropped her knitting into her lap.

"That's a better face," she said.

"Is it right to be this happy?" Tilly asked, hugging herself and spinning around in her delight.

"Everyone deserves to be happy," Mrs. Nugent said. "So when's the wedding to be?"

"Next Saturday," Tilly told her. "And I don't have to do a thing. It's all arranged."

The following week went by in a blur. Ryan took Tilly to introduce her to his family in Canmore, driving them in an automobile loaned by Mr. Brewster for the trip. Tilly went up to the hotel for wedding dress fittings and was treated to lunch by Burma and Mr. Evans. The more she saw of him, the more she liked him. One of the bridesmaids asked if Tilly would prefer to have one of her own friends take her place. The only person Tilly could think of was Fliss, who gratefully declined, preferring to remain in the background.

The morning of her wedding day, Tilly went up to Burma's room. She still could not quite believe that it was happening. The bridesmaids had gathered there too, primping hair and polishing nails. Despite only having just met them, they all treated her as one of them. One ran her a bath while another tipped scented bath salts into it. Tilly stepped into the tub, luxuriating in the warm water. At least it wouldn't be her responsibility to clean it today, she thought. After a long, relaxing soak, she finally stepped out of the tub, and wrapped herself into one of the hotel's fluffiest robes.

When she rejoined the group in the lounge, they swept her into the bedroom where they dressed her hair and applied her make-up. Having never worn much before, Tilly didn't know what to expect, but when she looked into the mirror a stranger looked back at her.

Her hair had been brushed back and fixed into a crown of curls on top of her head. Her face had been powdered and contoured with rouge to emphasise her cheek bones. Her eyes somehow looked bigger and bluer from the application of violet eye shadow and two coats of black mascara.

Burma stood behind her and smiled at her reflection.

"Beautiful," she murmured. "Just beautiful. And now for your traditional gifts."

"What are those?" Tilly looked up, astonished that there could possibly be more.

"Something old, something new, something borrowed, and something blue," the girls chorused.

"Here's something old." Lillian handed her a lace handkerchief. "It's antique lace from a street market in Marseilles."

"And here's something new." Frances gave her a little black box and, when Tilly opened it, she cried out in delight at the delicate pale pink pearl earrings laying there. "These are conch pearls, from the Bahamas."

Helen stepped up next and handed her a small, silver ring. "This is my own pinky ring for you to borrow. I should wear it on your right hand, and then it won't get in the way of your engagement ring and wedding band."

"And this," Ruth announced, "fresh from the sauciest lingerie store I could find in Rome, is something blue." She stretched a bright blue garter and let it go with a suggestive snap. "In ancient Rome, you know, blue was worn by brides as a symbol of love, modesty, and fidelity."

Tilly looked at the gifts, knowing they had been intended for Burma but now so willingly given to her. Her heart filled with gratitude and she could not speak.

"No crying now," Burma warned her. "We don't want to have to do your face all over again. Stand up and we'll help you into your dress."

Tilly stepped into the confection of layers of embroidered tulle over a satin underlay and pulled it up, slipping the diamante-studded spaghetti straps over her shoulders. Burma tugged the dress into place before closing the long back zip, which secured the close-fitting bodice in place. She stood to one side as Helen stepped forward to fit a satin band around Tilly's waist.

"Oh," Burma gasped when she saw the final result. "I had this dress modelled on one Ginger Rogers wore in the movie *The Gay Divorcee*. It is gorgeous. You are gorgeous, Tilly. I just hope I look as good on my wedding day."

Tilly slipped the handkerchief beneath her waist band, put the ring on her little finger and finally clipped on the earrings. The garter was already snug about her mid-thigh.

"And now for the *piece de la résistance*." Ruth stood on a step-stool and Tilly's heart hammered in her chest as the white, lace-edged, veil dropped over her head.

She held her breath as the filmy tulle cascaded over her shoulders. Ruth tweaked it and fluffed it until, smiling with satisfaction, she nodded approvingly.

"Come and take a look." She gently propelled Tilly towards the mirror again. When Tilly finally looked up, could not believe the vision before her.

She hardly recognized herself, so what would Ryan think of her? Would he see the girl he fell in love with, or this tall, regal stranger? Happiness shone in her eyes. Rose pink lipstick made her mouth look soft and inviting. For a moment Tilly wished her mother and father could see her, but then realized that if she could see a ghost, they must still exist somewhere. The thought comforted her.

Burma answered a knock on the door, and in came Mr. Evans, as handsome as ever in a gray suit over a white shirt with a white silk bow tie.

"I take it you're ready?" He smiled down at her.

"As I'll ever be," she said softly, taking the bouquet of white roses Burma handed her.

"Good girl," he said approvingly, and offered her his arm.

Tilly slipped her hand into the crook of his elbow, then looked up at him. "I don't know how to thank you and Burma for all of this."

Mr. Evans patted her hand. "You already did, my dear. I still have my daughter thanks to you. Now, are you ready to meet your groom?"

Tilly, suddenly a little shy, nodded. She was simply too happy to speak. Feeling as light as air, she walked beside Mr. Evans along the corridor to the stairs. They walked down each flight until the final flight that would take them to the ballroom. Tilly hesitated. Somewhere in her mind a voice said, "You won't fall", and she continued confidently down the stairs. People stopped to watch them pass, and then the ballroom doors opened. The strains of the wedding march rang out. Now the moment was here, her heart pounded even more and butterflies fluttered around in her stomach. She drew in a swift breath and then let it out again when she saw Ryan.

He stood by a bridal arch decorated in white roses at the far end of the ballroom. Billy and Pete stood beside him, all of them scrubbed clean, and dressed in their best suits. A bubble of laughter drove the butterflies away. None of them looked half as comfortable as they did in their work clothes. She clutched Mr. Evans's arm, grateful for the support, as they drew closer.

Everything she had lost seemed replicated here. Mr. Evans stood in for her father. She had gained a set of parents-in-law and another father and mother in George and Mrs. Nugent, who had taken to her as if she were their own. It looked like she might have acquired a set of brothers in Billy and Pete. She had more friends than she had ever thought possible, and now she was to have a husband of her own. She looked at Ryan and everything around her faded into the background as she saw the love in his eyes.

Mr. Evans lifted her veil and kissed her cheek.

"You look beautiful," he whispered. "I couldn't be more proud of you if you were my own daughter."

He gave her hand to Ryan and everything around her faded away as their fingers touched, grasped, then held. She didn't need him tell her that he loved her. She could see it in the warm glow in his eyes. Did she detect a tear there, too, or was it simply the shimmer of happiness blurring her own vision?

She had no recollection of speaking her lines, only of hearing herself say, "I do" and feeling the cool gold band Ryan slipped onto her finger. She only remembered her giddy relief when the minister said, "You may kiss the bride" and Ryan's lips covered hers.

When they broke apart and turned to face the room, she was shocked to see so many more people had come in. Miss Richards and Miss Taylor waved at her. Mr. Spence stood like a rock behind Miss Richards. Something in his stance made Tilly look again. He had just whispered something to Miss Richards, who blushed. She could almost forgive anyone anything today, and smiled a greeting as Mr. Spence stepped forward.

"It may not be the most appropriate time, Mrs. Blake," he said, "but I would like to advise you that we, that is Miss Richards and I, know you didn't steal Miss Turville's ring. Other items had gone missing during the duration of Mr. Vanderoosten's stay and now we have proof of his guilt."

"Has he been arrested?" Tilly's head spun a little that he had called her Mrs. Blake. She liked the sound of it.

"Not yet. A warrant has been issued for his arrest and Miss Evans is pressing further charges for assault on her person."

"Thank you for telling me, Mr. Spence. That is a wedding gift in itself." As he turned away, looking very pleased with himself, Tilly caught his arm and whispered, "Best of luck with Miss Richards."

His startled look made her laugh, but then she was surrounded by Saul and a crowd of bellhops who whooped and hollered around her. Tilly wondered who was taking care of the guests' luggage. Fliss wiped her eyes and Tilly had a pang of guilt that she had a wedding and a husband that she could share with the world.

When the speeches were done, when the frothy confection of a wedding cake had been cut, three gentlemen in dark suits walked into the ballroom and set up their music stands. Burma had already chosen the music to be played at her wedding and Tilly had only changed one piece.

As the first bars of the barcarolle drifted into the room, Tilly walked into the circle of Ryan's arms. She smiled up at him as he held her close and swayed with him as each step took them into the center of the ballroom. He spun her around and she leaned back against his arm, confident that he wouldn't let her slip, wouldn't let her go.

The music swelled and, as their guests began to join them on the floor, Tilly sensed a presence in that swirling, twirling crowd. Each time Ryan turned her, she looked over his shoulder, sure that her ghostly counterpart must be somewhere in the throng.

And then she saw her, dancing in the arms of a handsome, dark-haired, man. She no longer looked at Tilly, but up at her partner. As they passed by, Tilly saw that she was smiling, that her eyes were alight with love as she looked up at him.

That is how I feel, Tilly thought as she looked up at Ryan. Here was her own handsome man, someone to work with, to laugh and cry with, and spend the rest of her life with.

The End.

On Borrowed Time
Shell Shocked
The Buxton Chronicles Boxed Set

The date on Victoria Chatham's driver's licence says one thing but this young-at-heart grandma says another. She will read anything that catches her interest but especially historical and western romances. She loves all four-legged critters, particularly dog but is being converted into a cat lover by Onyx, an all black mostly Manx cat who helps her write. However, it's her passion for horses that gets her away from her computer to trail ride and volunteer at Spruce Meadows, a world class equestrian center near Calgary, Alberta, where she currently lives.

She loves to travel and spends as much time as she can with her family in England.